Mountain Man's FAKE FIANCE

DEE ELLIS

Mountain Man's Fake Fiancé by Dee Ellis
© 2022 by Dee Ellis. All rights reserved.
No part of this book may be reproduced in any written, electronic, recording, or photocopying without written permission of the publisher or author. The exception would be in the case of brief quotations embodied in the critical articles or reviews and pages where permission is specifically granted by the publisher or author.

Cover Design: Dee Ellis
Interior Formatting: Dee Ellis
Publisher: Hummingbird Press

Chapter One

Chapter Two

Chapter Three

Chapter Four

Chapter Five

Chapter Six

Chapter Seven

Chapter Eight

Chapter Nine

Chapter Ten

Epilogue

Thank You for Reading!

Chapter One

Brett

    Whoever thinks it is good to be me is an asshole.

    Once upon a time, in a former life, I thought I wanted to be famous. I thought I wanted to be adored and respected. I fought for gold and won and then I reaped the benefits of being someone people thought mattered. But at the end of the day, it didn't feel as good as I hoped.

    People hate me more than they love me. They call me cocky and detestable. I was voted least liked celebrity athlete. When I do interviews the main questions are about my short stint on a romance reality show. It was a gag to have a good time with some of my friends and meet some women. We had some fun, but I never expected to find a true love connection.

    And the truth is, I am not good with women. Not that good with people at all. My small circle of friends say I come across as rude. Standoffish. I say I just don't know how to talk to people one-one-one, so I don't. I can put on a show when it's called for. Turn off the cameras or take away my skis and I do not know how to act.

    Because cameras followed me for years, I was viewed as a spoiled, arrogant brat. After winning my first gold medal, the world was my oyster and I sucked it down. I partied, lived a jet-set lifestyle, and let the bright lights catch me doing it. Didn't take long to realize it was not life for me.

    Growing up all I cared about was being on the powder. Bombing down a mountain side or leaping off a jump and tricking in the air. It was the one thing I was good at, and I was damn good at it. I loved being out there on the snow and the excitement of hurtling off the mountain to hit the air and soar for a few moments.

    When my parents passed away when I was young, I wound up with my grandfather. He was a good man who taught me everything I know, but he was about as good with people as a grizzly bear. I guess that is where I get it. He also taught me about loving the freedom of being on a pair of skis.

    We lived in the mountains of Driftwood, Georgia, where he owned a small ski lodge that catered to the locals and tourists. Working there was the best time of my life, and I grew to love being on the mountain. I went pro when I was barely a teen because I knew it was all I would ever be good at.

"Where is your head at, Brett?" a voice breaks into my thoughts and I blink, taking note of where I am and why I am here.

"Lost in thought. Sorry," I shake myself as I apologize.

"No, I understand you do not want to be here. It's good for them to see you at these things so people see you as a...." Luke trails off when I cut in.

"As a spoiled and cocky man whore? I got it," I grumble, glancing out over the crowd sucking down the champagne and lobster pastries I paid for.

Luke will write all this excess off in the name of charity. I am hosting a holiday fundraiser here in Driftwood where it all started for me. Most of these folks considered me a bum most of my life because of where I came from and what I could and *could not* afford. Now they clamor to hang out at these parties to be seen with me.

Money means nothing to me. At least it doesn't now that I have plenty of it. Money *can* make you happier—whoever says it can't is a liar. It can pay your bills, put you in a nice house, get you a nice car, and take care of your family. It can make the things you worried about go away.

Money also brings out the worst in people.

"Well, half of them think that," Luke says with a chuckle.

"Which half?" I snort, glancing down from the balcony at the crowd.

I know which half thinks I am cocky and which half thinks I am a man whore. Most the men in this town hate me since half the women in town want me. I am not bragging when I say that—it's a fact I am not all that proud of. Good thing I stopped caring what people thought of me a long time ago.

When I feel the air in the room change, I can admit that is not true. There is one person whose opinion of me bothers me. Even with a room full of beautiful and classy socialites, I spot her like a diamond in the rough. I think she outshines every woman in the room.

Brielle North is the most beautiful sight I have ever laid eyes on. When I first saw her four months ago when I first got back home, I was awe-struck. It was my first time back at the lodge since I left Driftwood after grandfather passed. I couldn't bear to close the place, so my best friend Luke has been taking care of it. There she was, stumbling on her skis and laughing with a group of girls who looked as if they belonged on a runway, not a ski slope.

They were all beautiful, sure, some of Driftwood's elite. It was Brielle I could not get enough of. Her wavy auburn hair spilled down her back as she stomped around in her skis. Creamy porcelain skin without a hint of makeup glowed in the sunshine and her bright blue eyes were full of warmth and a touch of mischief. She was trouble with a capital T, I could tell.

Those friends of hers may have been laughing at her but it didn't faze her. With a beaming smile, she marched out to the lift and climbed on in her cute snow suit. I waited at the bottom of the hill for her, finding myself worried about her safety. Sure enough, she came racing down the hill and slammed right into me. I was glad to be the one to break her fall.

"Appreciate you being there, Ace," she had chortled as she sat astride me, both of us covered in snow.

Feeling her soft body in that puffy suit pressed against me felt too good. *Too right.* I tried to hold her even longer as I asked her name and if she wanted me to show her how to ski. I wanted nothing more than to spend the day on the mountain with her. When she pushed away, darkness churning in her light eyes, I sensed I had asked for too much.

"No thanks, Ace," she huffed as she sat straddling me. *"Don't need any help making a fool of myself."*

Before I could turn on the charm I was famous for, she was gone. It was refreshing she had no idea who I was. But she was going to find out. A little flirting with her friends *who did* know of me got me her name. For the first time, I used my so-called connections to find out about her.

Brielle comes from old money. Stupid big money. People claim she was a spoiled brat who blows money, makes a scene anywhere she goes, and won't be tamed. Most would write her off as just a spoiled princess.

And yeah, she blows money. Gives it away like her opinions. Only she gives it for the *right reasons*—and to the right people. Her and her besties, Quinn VonMuth and Lennon Baldwin are true philanthropists. They protest and march and even work at shelters. Life before they came to Driftwood was parties and paparazzi. They left that life behind a long time ago.

Making scenes—well she is hard to miss. Thick and curvy, with that crimson hair, beautiful eyes, and stunning face, heads turn wherever she goes. Maybe she is a bit of a princess—there is something regal about her. About the way she enters a room, head held high as her crystal blue eyes scan the space, looking for something or someone worthy of her interest.

Tonight, they land on me. When she catches me watching her, I can see her flush even from a distance. It strikes me as funny—she should be used to the way I watch her by now. I spent the past few months watching her. More often than she even knows. She is not here by mistake—I want her here.

"There she is," I say as my heart starts to beat differently. Luke is very aware of my obsession with Brielle. He had warned me she might not be here despite the invite I hand delivered to her two weeks ago. "I told you she would be here. Brielle knows I want her here."

Watching her move through the crowd, I never take my eyes off her. Lennon is with her—she knew better than to bring a date as her plus one. This is a fancier affair than I tend to host, with everyone dressed to impress. I tug at my own tux as I watch her gown light up the room.

Brielle is stunning in a wine-colored dress. Low cut on the front, with a sexy slit that showcases miles of leg, it is sexy as hell. When she turns to talk to Lennon, I see her back is bare but for a few flimsy straps. My hands itch to touch her, to trace the floral tattoo at her shoulder with my fingertips. As she turns to continue through the crowd, her skirt flares. From up here I can see her panties and immediately I want to rip them off to bare her.

"Fuck, she is so beautiful," I groan as I watch her charm everyone she passes.

"Yeah, she is," Luke agrees, throwing his hands up when I glare at him. "And I know just as everyone else does that she is off limits, so relax."

When I do relax, he laughs and shakes his head. I guess I have made it clear my intentions for her. Not that she seems to notice. I have tried to flirt with her, to find out what she likes or places she likes to go, but she ignores me. Unfortunately, Brielle sees me the same way others see her.

A spoiled brat who is not worth the effort.

Maybe once upon a time, I was that guy. Showing off on a reality show, being followed by paparazzi, and being a cocky prick did me no favors. Now I host charity events like this, I spend my time dodging cameras while I am doing good instead of showing off for them. Which means no one knows that I turned over a new leaf, but I don't care what most people think.

But *I do* care what Brielle thinks of me.

"I am going to go talk to her," I announce as a wave of panic hits me. Any charm I showed playing a ski stud vanishes once I see her. I tried a dozen times to talk to her just to make a fool of myself. To ask her out or get her number or something...just to walk away with a bruised ego.

Rushing down the stairs, I stumble twice but catch myself before I face plant. I could soar on skis but in these wingtips, I am a disaster. Fixing my tie, I square my shoulders and mentally rehearse what I want to say. I mean I can't really tell her all the things I want to.

I cannot tell her I am borderline obsessed with her. Or that I would do anything or give anything to spend time with her. To know what goes on in that head of hers. To find out what makes her smile. And to be the person who makes her happy. The one who gets to take care of her.

"Evening, Brielle," I manage as I approach her, fixing my suit and fussing with my tie again. "You look...you look...just, wow," I stutter.

Rolling my eyes at myself as she turns to face me, I wait for her to dismiss me. We have done this dance before. I get the courage to talk to her and she blows me off. Things won't go down that way tonight. I am going to ask her out. I want her to give me a chance to show her I can be good to her.

"Thank you, Ace," she offers as she tilts a look up at me. Her eyes sparkle in the dim lighting of the room. Makes her look as if she is keeping a secret. And she lets me in on her secret. "Looking good yourself, Brett."

My insides churn at the way she looks at me as she says my name. It's just the second time she has ever used it. Usually, she just calls me Ace, which I hate. Seems too impersonal. This feels...very personal. As her eyes slide over me, heat floods the space between us, and I step closer.

"Thanks. You really look beautiful," I whisper as I reach for her hand. I draw it to my lips and press a soft kiss to the silky skin of her wrist. Her eyes flash and her pulse thumps beneath my lips. Good. That's a good sign.

"Thank you," she whispers, her voice as soft as satin.

Keeping hold of her hand, I toy with her fingers absently. I tug her closer and she comes, surprising me. Her sweet scent hits me and I am dazed. Strawberries and something fresh. Soap or rain. I dip my head, so my nose touches the top of her head, and breathe her in, smiling when she giggles.

"Awful forward tonight, Ace," her voice rasps sexily, making my dick jerk.

"Am I being forward? Greeting you like a lady, remarking how stunning you look...is that forward?"

"It is for you," she husks, tipping her head back to gaze up at me.

Something simmers in the air between us. It's different than the one-sided need that I have felt every single time I get close to her. I blink in shock, stunned it hits me the way it does. Her light eyes watch me with a heat I have never seen before. Heat I very much want to explore.

"Surprised you came," I whisper softly, wanting to keep this intimacy I feel between us going.

"You knew I would," she husks back with a wicked smile. "I am a sucker for charities."

Tilting my head at her, I wonder if she means the charities, we are here raising money for. Or if she means me, a charity case slightly obsessed with her. When she smirks at me, I think it might be the latter, but I don't care.

I will take her charity if it means getting what I want—and *I want her.*

Chapter Two

Brielle

High society has no idea what a bore it is.

Growing up with money should make life easier. In some ways it did, of course. I went to the best schools, was able to see the world on holidays, and had a black card that never ran out of spending money. It left me isolated from the world. I was only allowed to talk to others like me—most of whom I could not stand.

My father was a powerful man who loved me and my brother but had little time for us. My mother passed when I was young, and he sent us off to be taken care of by strangers. My brother was all I had left so being separated was extremely hard for me. I felt discarded during the formative years of my life.

Quinn VonMuth saved me from complete isolation during our time at boarding school. We were roommates with Lennon Gallo, the three of us becoming as thick as thieves during our years there. If not for the two of them, I may not have survived my miserable youth.

With the two of them leading the way, I started to figure myself out. I am not my mother, a regal prima donna who loved the lifestyle my father provided her. And as much as I loved my brother Caleb, I was not driven to succeed the way he was.

All I ever wanted was to be proud of who I was and what I did.

It took some time to get there but I am both. Once I finished college to please my father, I took some time to decide what I was going to do next. During that time, I saw a different world than the one I had grown up in.

With Quinn and Lennon leading the way, I witnessed the struggles and strife others suffered. While we flew on private jets and were chauffeured in sleek limousines, too many went hungry and homeless. We decided we had to do something—because we had the means to make a difference.

Trading private jets for electric cars and less carbon footprints, we did what our fathers before us said they would. We gave back. To homeless havens and animal shelters. We marched for equal rights and pushed for those rights to become laws. Our travels were not to fashion shows or exotic islands but to rebuild war-torn villages and fund water supplies systems.

Our work together has been rewarding but risky—but I am proud of all we accomplished together.

"Thoughtful Brielle means *a nervous* Brielle," Lennon's voice singsongs playfully as I am snapped from my thoughts.

Frowning at her, I turn away, so a curtain of crimson hair hides my face. Because she will see me flush and that will give me away. I am nervous. It is not a foreign feeling, I spent most of my life nervous. Nervous about letting my father down or stepping out of my brothers' shadow.

This is not that sort of nervous. No, this is a feeling reserved for just one thing—seeing Brett Shea. A feeling so overwhelming for me that I avoid it at all costs. Or rather, I *avoid him* at all costs. Being anywhere near him is not a good idea for me because I am reduced to a simpering idiot.

"Why would I be nervous to eat free food and donate money to a good cause?" I counter, finally glancing at my best friend as I tuck my hair over my shoulder. Before I finish telling the lie, it falls back in my face again.

"What cause again, Bri? You don't remember. Once you saw who was hosting this shindig, you were all in. Tell me I am wrong," she challenges as our heels click on the sidewalk, her taunt making my temper flare.

On a crisp November evening we are dressed to kill. Could be just another night out in the big city. Nights here in Driftwood are nothing like even the best nights in the city. Since coming here last spring, I have grown to love the little town for all its wonder. It's the most beautiful place I have ever been, and I have been just about everywhere.

When we came here, it was to protest a logging company we were convinced were wrecking the landscape. We quickly found out how wrong we were because they might be the most socially conscious company we have ever tried to protest. It was the best mistake we ever made.

Because Quinn found the love of her life when she met Keller, the foreman of the site we came to protest. Unable to break up the trio, we decided to stick it out here in Driftwood with her. It was the best decision of my life. Until I laid eyes on one tall, dark slice of trouble.

"Watch your mouth, Len," I growl at her playfully as I scan the room looking for that delicious slice. I have not admitted to myself or anyone else that I came here tonight looking for him. Not that I need to admit a thing to Lennon—she knows me well enough to know I am here looking for trouble.

"Well, well, looking for you as usual," she teases, shoving me gently.

Glancing up, I spot him. And he is looking for me. He always seems to be looking for me, but I have tried to keep my distance. I am not particularly good at it because I don't actually want that distance, I force between us. And he does not make it easy because he made it very clear he wants zero distance.

Brett is bright, beautiful, and *way* wrong for me. He got famous for being a ladies' man on a bad bachelor show a few years ago. While he never found his happy ever after, he seemed to have an awful lot of fun trying to. Not that I watched the show—I was too busy marching for rainforests.

"They did that man dirty," Lennon whisper shouts beside me, "cameras cannot capture how totally hunky he is."

"Do you enjoy breathing?" I turn to glare at her, "If so, stop talking. I am not here for him. Neither of us are."

Lennon laughs at me, and I hide my smirk. Way to pretend I am not pissed at her for saying how hot he is. I am fully aware of how hot he is. I have spent months trying to ignore that hotness. Ignore how I feel when he looks at me with those amber eyes. He looks at me as if I am the only girl in the world. I should love it, but it just scares me.

How do you trust a man who lived out a dozen romances for the world to see?

"Stop it. We came to eat," Lennon waggles her brows as she eyes me salaciously, "or maybe to *get* eaten."

"Len! Always a pervert," I laugh though because how can I not?

As I am laughing, I feel the air shift. It always heats and crackles whenever Brett is close. His presence takes up all the space around me as he moves closer than he should. When the warmth of his palm presses to my back, I close my eyes and take a deep breath. He always touches me when we see each other, and I am no longer able to pretend I don't like his touch.

"Evening, Brielle," his husky voice is close to my ear as he greets me. "You look...you look...just, wow," he stutters a bit, and I cannot help but grin at how damn adorable he is.

When I turn to face him, I am not prepared. He always looks handsome in his suits or even jeans and sweaters. Tonight, he looks.... amazing. His fitted tux shows how big and broad he is. His tie is crooked, but I think it's perfect. His golden eyes shine in the dim lighting of the room and when he smiles at me, that dimple that drives me crazy pops and I almost swoon.

"Thank you, Ace," I manage before I compose myself. "Looking good yourself, Brett."

Watching him flush pink makes my heart turn over. *God he is so cute.* Well, really, he is beautiful with his straight nose and strong jaw. His smile flashes his perfect white teeth before his tongue comes out, swiping sensually over his full mouth. Lord, that mouth. It's sinfully hot, full, soft bottom lip, perfect sexy top lip.

Brett grins down at me, reaching out to take my hand. I let him because I am so stunned by him tonight, I forget I am supposed to be pushing him away, not letting him pull me close. He lowers his head, brushing a kiss at my wrist. My pulse thrums against his lips and his eyes flash because he feels it. Dammit. I flush and glance away, but I don't pull my hand away.

His grin widens and he laces his fingers with mine, I know I am in trouble. My palm presses against his and our hands fit together perfectly. A cyclone of heat races up my arm and settles in my chest. He pulls me closer, and I let him, making cute banter with him that I always refuse us.

Before I know it, we are headed for the glimmering dance floor as slow melodies play. I don't know how it happens, but I wind up pressed against his chest, his palm at my back. I lay my head on his shoulder as if we have done this a dozen times. It feels too right to be wrapped in his arms. To feel him sway us to the music as I his scent and the firmness of his strong arms around me wraps around me.

It feels as if I am floating on air, not dancing with a famous playboy.

We dance to half a dozen songs before I notice people are watching us. Others dance with us but circle around as if watching us put on a show. I start to pull away because I hate having eyes on me, but he tenses. I tilt my head back to see distress on his face. My heart pitter-pats again.

"Don't go," his voice is pained, and I blink up at him. Brett lowers his head until his brow touches mine.

"Stop," the word punches out of me along with my breath. His eyes close and he shakes his head, starting to back away. Once his warmth is gone, I feel panic bubbling beneath my surface. My eyes circle the room looking for something to calm me. When I come up empty, I reach out to him, dragging him back. He lets out a rumbling sound, his hands closing at my waist to pull me close.

"You asked me to stop. But you won't *let me* stop," he whispers, and I know he means more than this back and forth tonight.

He means all the time since we met at his ski lodge, and I blew him off. I was so overwhelmed when I first saw him, waiting at the bottom of the slope I was careening down. When he broke my fall, he just flashed that stunning smile of his and offered to show me how to survive on skis. I thought he was making fun of me after I'd made a fool of myself.

Later, when I found out who he was—a professional skier who could ski circles around everyone on that mountain—I really felt like a fool. When I heard about his little reality romance show, I saw him for what he was. Another hot shot heartbreaker who loved attention and accolades.

Once again though, it seems my first impression was wrong. He may have filled a playboy role for the cameras, but he seems anything but. Brett can be found one of two places: his ski lodge, keeping his grandfather's dream alive or brooding in the coffee shop in town. Well, three places—lately he seems to be just about anywhere I am.

After we met at the lodge, I tried to ignore him. I tried to pretend all those times we wound up at the same place were mere coincidence. And I tried to tell myself that his fumbling flirtations were passing fancy. But no matter how often I brush him off or push down what he makes me feel, there he seems to be, waiting for another shot.

"You don't mean tonight, do you?" I ask him to confirm my suspicions.

"No, bunny, I don't mean tonight," his voice is rough and sexy as he whispers these words against my ear.

My hands clutch at his jacket, and I realize I am pulling him closer. I want to push him away at the same time I can't let go of him. He scares me. He rattles my senses and I hate that. I swore I would never be like my mother who devoted her life to her family and never lived for herself.

Something about him makes me wonder things I never thought I would. About weddings and me in a white dress and him in a tux. I close my eyes now and can imagine this is us sharing our first dance as husband and wife. It is beautiful to picture it and pretend it could happen.

Of course, I know better—Brett Shea is not the guy who settles down. Good thing Brielle North is not a girl looking to settle down.

Chapter Three

Brett

Holding Brielle feels like taking a hold of my future.

We dance to half a dozen songs, and she lets me hold her as close and as tight as I want. Truth is, I don't want to let her go. Not when it is the first time she has let me get this close. Usually, we flirt a little before she shuts me down, pretending she does not enjoy this back and forth as much as I do.

Tonight, I called her out on it. When she started to pull away, I panicked. I was drowning in her sweet scent and soft curves. I was not ready to let her go, so I begged her not to go. I may have sounded pathetic, but I don't care. I will beg for her, I will plead, I will get down on my knees if that is what she demands.

Whatever it takes to make her mine—whether it be romantic flowers or candies or diamonds and gold—whatever it takes.

"Why did you call me bunny?" she whispers as we sway to another song.

Easing my hands over her hips and up her back, I smile. I have called her that more than once, but she never seemed to notice before. Tonight, she seems very attuned to me, shifting her body closer whenever I pull away. I test this out by pulling back to answer her. To my pleasure, she lets out a sound of protest and presses closer, locking her arms around my neck.

"That day we met," I answer, sliding my hand to the nape of her neck to tilt her head back. "You came crashing down that slope. I thought you were beautiful and brave. You did not belong on that slope," I say with a chuckle, smiling when she flushes. "You should have been on the bunny slope."

Brielle laughs and I feel my chest warm at that beautiful sound. She burrows her face against my neck, and I leave my fingers tangled in her silky hair. We've forgotten the rest of the crowd. I don't even care about the auction we will be hosting tonight. I don't want to stop twirling around the room with my sweet bunny in my arms.

"I like it," her voice floats just above the music and I grin.

"Good. I won't call you anything else," I rasp back as my fingers slip into her hair to tilt her head back again.

Her eyes flash up at me, dark with heat and I feel my dick jerk. She may have kept me at a distance all these months, but her eyes told me she didn't want to. Now they tell me everything I want to know. They tell me she is turned on, just like I am, and that she doesn't want me to let her go.

"Brett," her voice is raspy, rough, her eyes glittering in the dim light of the ballroom we keep spinning around.

"Yes, bunny?" I reply as I lower my head so close that my lips almost touch hers.

"They keep calling for you," There is nothing but nerves in her voice now and I frown, hating that something is intruding on us.

"What? Who is calling?" I turn to glance at the stage where Luke is waiting, eyes trained on me as he waits for me to snap out of it. He tells a bad joke about skiers being thick skulled and I toss a few choice words his way.

Turning back to Brielle, I hesitate. Lowering my head again, I touch my nose to hers, darting my tongue out to trace her mouth. Her soft moan makes my dick surge in my slacks, and I groan. "Don't you go away, bunny. I will be back for you."

Her breath pants against my mouth and I smile, knowing I affected her. Striding towards the stage with the whole room watching makes me very aware of how hard I am in my fitted tux. When I glance back, Brielle is where I left her, watching me take the stage. I grin at her, and wink and I wish I could see her in the low lights because I know she is flushed.

"Here he is folks," Luke announces as he steps back from the podium, inviting me to take his place.

"Thank you," I call out to the crowded room, chuckling nervously when the mic crackles and a titter of laughs moves through the room.

Glancing out at the crowd I note very few familiar faces. Mostly strangers who want to be seen giving money to charities. Over the holiday season there will be several of these sorts of shindigs. All of these people, myself included, will be expected to be there to open our wallets.

When my gaze lands on Brielle, I am hit with inspiration. I will go to each and every charity event this season—because I know she will be there. These things are profoundly important to her—and I want to make it an important part of my life too. I want to be a better man for her. Because of her.

"Open those clutches, unfold those money clips, bid on some wonderful, unique items from some of my friends, and bid big. This is for charities who need your funds to get through the holidays. Spend it like you mean it."

Brielle grins up at me and I flush, nodding my head at her. I leave Luke to it and go to join her. He explains the many items up for auction tonight, from signed snowboards from me and my former Olympic teammates, season tickets to the Harmony Hollow Hawks football team, and even designer jewelry from Rian Thorn.

Bidding starts, and I watch Luke score thousands of dollars for our favorite charities. One percent of the sales will go to Shea Ski Lodge, to fund the operation of the place, but besides that, every single dime will go to those charities. It feels good to give something back.

"How much is too much for that very nice snowboard, signed by the infamous Brett Shea?" Brielle teases beside me when Luke announces it.

"Bunny," my voice is rough as I watch her eyes dance, her hand going up slowly. "Maybe you would prefer a private one-on-one lesson with the man himself? No need to bid, I would be yours for free," I tell her, heat sizzling in the air between us.

Her chin lifts as her arm goes up higher, her fingers flicking. Luke spots her bid and calls it out. I reach out, grabbing her hip to draw her close. Her hand wiggles again, upping her bid. My hand drifts lower, cupping her plump ass and she bites her lip. Another flick of her hand. I grip her ass in my hand and yank her against me as she laughs, upping her bid once again.

Luke calls it at four grand but someone else is outbidding her. Bending my head, I brush my lips over her ear, telling her to stop bidding. I promise to get her a matching board. She makes another bid, raising it to six grand. When I promise to take her on the bunny slope and tell her why I really call her bunny, she whimpers and nods, flicking her hand again. Eight grand.

"Brielle, stop it," I growl, swatting her ass and grunting when she moans. "I will give you what you want, Bunny. Just ask me."

"I want that board, Ace," she purrs against my throat before she stuns me, licking a fiery path up my throat to my ear. "I don't want someone else to get it. *I want it.* Don't you want me to have it?" her voice is hot honey as it drips over me and I grip her ass tighter, letting her feel how badly I want her to have it. Her tits are soft, but I feel the pebbled nipples through her silky dress.

"I want you to have it, bunny," I growl, sliding my hand up to tangle it in her hair. Yanking her head back, I press my mouth to her ear. "Keep bidding. Show me how bad you want it, baby." Our bodies press tightly together as I fist her hair at the nape of her neck, watching her beam up at me with a sexy smirk, her eyes sparkling.

"Thirteen thousand," her voice rings out above the other bidding, the entire room quieting with a hush.

"Sold," Luke shouts, slamming his gavel down as he grins at us.

"It's yours, bunny," I whisper against her throat as she laughs.

"Is it, ace?" she taunts me, biting her bottom lip as she gazes up at me.

Without thinking about what ought to come next, I back out of the room, pulling her with me. I do not care if people know we left or figure out why I am sneaking off with her. All I care about is getting my mouth on her. Hearing her sounds as I please her. Brielle's walls went down tonight. I want to wreck those walls so she can no longer put them up to keep me out.

"Bunny, we need to be alone," I insist as I lead her down a dark stairwell to a hall lit by a stone fireplace. It is quiet, warm, and dark as I spin to press her to the stone wall.

"Brett," her voice pants as I slide my knee between hers, caging her in with my palms against the river rock wall behind her. "I... I hate what you do to me. But I love it too," she whimpers, reaching up to grab my jacket, yanking me closer.

Unable to hold back, I dip my head and slam my mouth against hers. Her moan vibrates against my mouth, and I lick her lips, groaning when she opens her mouth. Grasping at her, I suck at her tongue and savor the sweetness of her. We kiss until we can't breathe and even then, I press tiny kisses to her swollen lips, her jaw, her face, not wanting to stop tasting her.

"Tell me what I do to you," I urge her even as my hands grip her dress, pulling it up until I can feel her thick thighs beneath my fingers.

"You...you scare me because you look at me like...you look at me as if I am the...."

"The only girl in the world. Because *you are*, Bunny," I rasp as I walk my fingers up the silkiness of her thighs, higher, slowly higher, until I find the tiny lace covering her.

"No, no," she argues, her head falling back against the wall as she glares up at me. "If I recall, there were about dozen before me, Ace."

Seeing jealousy flare in her beautiful eyes hits me right in the chest. It tells me she does feel something for me. That these months we've done this back-and-forth dance was not for nothing. I hate that I did that stupid show even if I did it for a good reason. And I hate that it bothered her because that means there is hope for us.

"Oh, bunny," I hum, fisting her panties in my hand, "is that what this is? That stupid show? It was for this place," I admit, rubbing my fingers over her folds, "to get people coming to my grandpa's place. To get people love it the way I do."

Brielle watches me for a moment, as if gauging what I said. As if she is considering I may speak the truth. Her eyes flash hot, her teeth nip at her bottom lip, and her hips shift slightly. Just enough to tell me not to stop what I started. Watching her, giving her a chance to stop me, I pull at her panties.

"It was all I had," I go on as I let the lace slide down her thighs, my hand moving to cup her sex. "My home. My legacy. I would have done just about anything for it to come back to life. Even make an ass out of myself."

"Oh...Oohh," she whimpers as I stroke her folds, finding them wet and sticky a I spread them open.

"Silky wet, bunny," I rasp, watching my fingers rub at her clit as her hips wriggle, her hands gripping the stones behind her. "I want to eat you. I want to lick that pretty pussy until you come on my face," I grunt, watching her cream drip down my fingers as I pump them inside her.

Before she can voice a response, I grasp her by her waist and settle her back on the stairs. Her legs fall open and I kneel between them as she grips the stairs above her. One of her hands comes to the back of my head and she nods her head, letting me lift one of her thighs at my shoulder.

"Yes, yes," she chants, nodding again, "yes, please, I want that. I want it too...oh...oh yes," she moans her words on a stuttering cry as I suck her clit into my mouth.

My fingers still pump inside of her, and I press down on her pelvis, to still her wriggling body. Her moans as I eat her make me so hard, I am sure I'm going to bust my zipper. But I don't care about my cock. I care about getting her off. About watching her come the way I have dreamt a hundred times since I first laid eyes on her.

When my teeth scrape across her pearl, her eyes roll back and she shouts, slamming her hand on the stairs. I shove my tongue inside her as she comes, suckling at her dew like an addict taking a hit. And *I am* an addict. I am addicted to her sugary pussy—and it is a habit I won't ever break.

"Brett," she murmurs my name so soft, so sweet, combing her hands through my hair.

"Yes, bunny," I husk back, kissing at her cleft, at each thigh, and at her soft tummy.

"I think you ruined me," she mutters, sitting up and tugging me between her legs. Her mouth covers mine and I haul her against me as we kiss ourselves breathless once again.

Setting her on her feet, I kiss her bare shoulders, whispering soft words to her. Telling her how beautiful she is. How breathtaking. I tell her I was ruined the moment I saw her. Brielle giggles at that and I sigh, watching her beam up at me with her beautiful smile.

"Come, bunny. I need to be there for the rest of the auction. After that...I am taking you home," I tell her, grasping her chin with my thumb.

For just a moment, I think she may deny me. I think that these moments here in this dark stairwell may be all I get to have with her. I fear she may remember how to put those walls back up no matter what I made her feel just now. Brielle's beaming smile never wavers as she nods just once.

"You can do that, Ace. You did promise to give me lessons on that board."

"I did promise, bunny. And I never break a promise," I tell her softly.

Brielle gazes up at me and I realize I need to prove that to her. I need to prove I won't ever break a promise I make her. Because I want to make her lots of promises.

Promises of a future, a family, and a forever together.

Chapter Four

Brielle

Spending a small fortune never felt so good.

After the hottest hookup of my life, I feel as if I float across the ballroom floor. With the auction over, people are claiming their items and bragging about how much they helped the charities. Really, they helped themselves because they want those trinkets more than they want to help.

But I am thrilled with my purchase. One of Brett's boards from a winter Olympics when he won gold. I almost bid on the skis he posed nude with for a cover of a magazine. Figured that would be too on the nose. I was doing my best to keep this man at a distance, but he just keeps closing that distance.

What we just shared in the darkness of that stairwell made me forget why I ever pretended I did not want him. I *do* want him. Though I spent months pretending I did not like his flirting or his attention, I did. *I do.*

"You will give me that lesson, won't you Ace?" I tease as we round the room, watching others gossip and gloat over their baubles.

"Of course, bunny," he purrs that cute pet name for me and a shiver of emotion rattles through me.

"You mean it," I say soberly, peering up at him as he beams down at me. Brett means what he says. He will teach me to ski because I asked him to. He said he is taking me home later and I know he means that too. Another little shiver shoots through me—equal parts alarm and awareness.

"I do," he answers steadily, his eyes never leaving mine. "I will do whatever you ask."

Something flashes in his eyes as the air between us changes. He means that. He means that whatever I ask, he will make sure it happens. I wonder as I stare up at him why I forced that distance between us. Why did I blow him off for all these months?

"Will you really take me home tonight?" I whisper softly, not wanting to share this moment with the others crowding the room.

"Yeah, bunny," he husks, lifting his hand to cradle my face, "I am taking you home tonight. To my home. Where I have wanted you since we met."

His golden eyes glitter with heat and I almost swoon. I press closer, sliding my hand up to cover his heart. It pounds beneath my hand and his hand tightens on my waist, tugging me even closer. It's indecent how we behave towards each other, but neither of us seems to care.

Grabbing my wrist, he brings it to his lips, kissing it the same way he did when I first got here. Only now his mouth has touched my mouth, my body, and made me come. There is something so sensual about the way he drags his lips over my skin, and I know my pulse is thumping.

"Come, let's get your prize. Sooner we get done here, the sooner I get you home," he taunts, wetting his bottom lip in a move so sexy I stumble in my heels.

Brett chuckles, catching me and walking me to the pay station. I tug my black card out of my lacy thigh-highs, and he lets out a growl that makes my lady parts swoon. God, he is so sexy. What was I thinking staying away for so long? *I was not thinking*, I tell myself—I was reacting.

Reacting to how confused I was by his attraction to me. Being cautious based on all the rumors I had heard about him. Whispers said he was cocky, rich, spoiled...and slutty. Foolishly I listened to others instead of paying attention to how his attention has been focused solely on me since we met

Handing my card over to the woman handling the purchases, I turn back to him. I press close, gazing up into his pretty eyes. His dimple flashes as he presses a hand to my back, pulling me as close as he can fit me. Heat simmers between us as we stand there, ignoring the rest of the world.

"You hungry, bunny?" his voice is deep, rough, and I am not certain if he means it salaciously, but the glimmer in his eyes tells me he does.

"Starving actually," I shoot back as I run my hand up his chest, touching each of the buttons on his tux.

"Excuse me," an icy voice breaks the spell we are under, "ma'am, I apologize.... this is no good," she sneers the words as a grin twists her ruby lips, her cold eyes narrow as they size me up.

"Pardon me? No good? How is it no good? It spends the same way cash does, sweetheart." Shame and anger wash over me as people turn to stare.

"It's a black card, Greta." Brett is there to rescue me, "of course it is good. Those cards have no limit, you know as well as I do. Do it again."

He moves behind me and pulls me back against his chest. He is there to protect me. I press back against him because I feel so safe with him there beside me. I do not know how or why we slipped into this so easily, but it feels right. It may have taken me some months to get here, but here I am.

We watch sour face Greta give that shiny black card another swipe. I am shocked when an offensive beep sounds as it reads *DECLINED*. I frown and reach out to take it from her. It is my company—well, my father's company—card and he is right, there is no limit.

Our money is old money—our families were men of industry, so I know nothing else. Father sits atop a throne of pomp and prestige. While his title is CEO of North Tech, that is just a title. His nephews and my brother do all the work. They design the software and the hardware that keeps my father and their fathers filthy rich.

"Take mine," Brett barks behind me, throwing his card at her when she continues to sneer at me.

"Brett, no," I gasp the words, turning to argue with him. "I can afford it. It must be an issue with father's accounts," I mumble, shame flushing me.

"Bunny, stop," he softens his voice, cradling my face in his hand. "It is for charity. Who cares where it comes from?"

I do, I think. To spare us more embarrassment, I say nothing. I allow him to pay as I stay silent at his side. They begrudgingly pass me my precious board and dismiss us both. I glare at Greta because this entire event is because of Brett. All these pretty trinkets were donated because of him. Here she is pretending to be the evil witch of Driftwood, looking down her pointy nose at someone giving to charity.

Letting him lead me out, I bow my head as we pass the crowd, feeling ashamed. I am not sure for what. When we get outside, he has a car waiting. Just before we start to climb in, I remember I came with Lennon. I start to turn back when he stops me.

"Lennon left earlier, bunny," he tells me calmly, smiling gently. "I made sure she got home safe. Come, I promised to take you home too, baby."

His voice is warm, and it both turns me on and calms me down. I let him load me into the back of the waiting town car, still a little rattled. When he climbs in, a veil of shyness falls over me. How does he do this to me? How does he reduce a former wild child who danced on bars and flirted with billionaires or even kings into a simpering fool?

Brett slides close and his woodsy cologne mixed with his clean linen smell invades my senses. I press even closer, watching his hand walk up my thigh and spread apart the split in my dress. His fingers trace the edge of my stockings, where the black card I tried to use moments ago is tucked.

"What went on back there, Brielle?" he presses as his fingers tease the fragile lace.

"Greta seemed displeased with me," my tone is as dry and curt as hers was. "Maybe she wanted what I got?" I taunt playfully, reaching my hand up to the back of his head to let my fingers sink into his silky hair.

"Bunny is there something going on? Is there something I can do?"

Brett seems genuinely concerned and it both endears me and angers me. I am not a woman who likes to depend on others. Even though I have always depended on my father's money, I earned it my own way. I did research and development in the field whenever we were chasing down another cause. I delivered legitimate data to my brother and cousins that had helped broaden our reach to South America, Australia, and parts of New Zealand.

"Last time I spoke with my father," I start cautiously, "he was on a kick about me coming back home. Settling down. Giving him grandbabies. I told him none of the above was going to happen."

We roll through the streets of Driftwood, the cool night lit with a canopy of twinkling stars. Holiday lights have already begun to glitter on Main Street with plenty of homes decked out like adorable gingerbread houses. It is my first winter here in Driftwood and the first holiday me and the girls have stayed in one place long enough to celebrate.

Lennon and I share an adorable little place on the edge of town. We decided just this week that we were going to put up a Christmas tree this weekend. It is the first time we have settled anywhere for long, so we are all excited about a real small-town holiday season. I told my father I would not be coming home anytime soon—if ever.

As if he can hear me being rebellious, my phone rings with my father's number lighting up the screen. I am tucked close against Brett when I realize his calls always make me anxious. He makes me feel worthless when he compares me to my brother. Having Brett there beside me makes me feel strong and I take the call, my shoulders going back and my chin lifting.

"Hello," I greet in a neutral tone, feeling Brett lock his thick arms around me as if he senses I need his support.

"Ginger thought I should call after another of your expenses showed up tonight." No greeting or how are you, and the mention of his assistant who I know he has been having an affair with puts me on edge. "We put a stop to it. Hope it did not embarrass you too much."

"No, not at all," I lie as I glance up at Brett. "Although it would be nice to be told about expense limits. Have I not done my part for the company again, Father?" My voice sounds detached even to my own ears.

"You have not done your part for this family, Brielle. You ought to be married by now with children. Your brother will be getting married soon. We expect you to be there," he clears his throat as he says we because he means *he and Ginger* expect me there. My brother has not mentioned being engaged any of the times we have talked lately. I frown and move even closer to Brett, almost wishing I could use him to shield me from whatever this is.

"Would have loved to have known so I could have been there to celebrate. Of course, I will be there for my brother's wedding," I snap.

"When you come, I expect you to announce your own engagement. I want you two wed as soon as possible. It looks bad for our brand for my children to be as old as they are, unwed, without children, globetrotting."

"I am twenty-four, not forty-four," I respond dryly, shaking my head. "And your son has been at your side building that brand. Just because I travel to do my part and do some good for our brand does not mean I do not do my part. You cannot tell me when to get married. My personal life has nothing to do with our business."

"To me, it does. I do nothing that might threaten our brand. You have done your charitable deeds and sowed your wild oats long enough, Brielle. It is time to return home and do your part here. I won't fund another trip, another shopping spree, or another extravagant purchase."

"Wait...wait. You mean to tell me I have to come home and get married.... or you want to just cut me off?" My voice trembles as I speak because I know that is just what he is doing.

"Cut you off is right. I am done funding your lifestyle. No more black card, no more allowances, no more money siphoned from this business. Not when you do nothing to earn it!"

"Father, *I have* earned what I spend. And I have a trust fund from grandaddy that you cannot control." My words echo in the small-town car that I realized has parked and sits outside of Brett's place.

"A trust fund you cannot touch until you turn twenty-five. With the way you like to live, I presume you will recognize your need to come home."

Stunned by his demands, I don't hear what he says for a few moments. I just sit there, staring up at Brett, tears blurring his beautiful face. I am not a spoiled brat the way the media has portrayed me. I worked for what I spend, just as I argued. And I handled all the philanthropic duties for our brand. I may have been a bit overzealous with that because I wanted to do good, but I was not taking trips and shopping like a trust fund baby.

Ending the phone call, even as my father continues to state demands, I press closer to Brett. With shaking hands, I skim through all my accounts. All of them have been frozen. I have no money. I have no way to live here in Driftwood. No money to pay rent at the cute place Lennon and I share or to cover the bare necessities.

"Oh my god!"

I am flat broke after foolishly spending thirteen grand on a snowboard.

Chapter Five

Brett

Being a good guy gets you nowhere, so I decide to be a bad guy.

It may be selfish of me to swoop in when Brielle is needy, and that makes me the bad guy. I am ok with that. The bad guy gets the girl in the movies and those dirty books all the ladies love. I will be the bad guy to get Brielle. Hearing her father has cut her off until she agrees to get married both enrages me and excites me.

It means I get a shot to be her hero even if it makes me a bad guy.

"Oh my god! My father cut me off—everything is gone!"

"Calm down, bunny," I murmur as we sit in the back of the town car.

Hearing her end of her uncomfortable conversation with her father made me irate. He thinks he can force her to get married to fulfill some role for their brand. Not just is that a demeaning demand, it is not an option—no one will be marrying off Brielle if I have a say in it.

Even considering her being married to someone else seems impossible.

In the past few months, I have thought of her a hundred ways. Thought of her in my bed, waiting for me to please her. I have thought of her round with my child, those stunning eyes of her shining with joy. And I have thought of her in white gown, waiting to promise me forever.

Her father boxing her into a corner works to my advantage. Tonight, I decided I was going to convince her to give dating me a shot. To forget about the playboy persona I put on for the cameras. I planned to propose she be my plus one for this holiday season at the many events we will be expected at.

"How can I calm down? Brett...I was a bit spoiled for my entire life—I never worked, *worked*, I never had to pay bills. I just...if he cuts me off, I don't know what to do."

Brielle sounds frantic and it pisses me off. Her father has no idea who he is dealing with. I may not come from old money, but I have powerful connections all the same. I will use them to destroy him if he tries to hurt her again.

He can cut her off from the family fortune—but I can make sure she never misses a dime of that money.

"Trust me, Brielle. Let me take care of things," I offer gently, brushing her crimson hair away from her face. I thumb away her tears and bend my head, brushing my lips across hers gently.

Touching her, kissing her, feeling her, it's better than money or power. It is better than winning gold. Being this close to her, smelling her perfume and her silky skin, feeling her heart thunder against my chest as I draw her close, it's better than any feeling I have ever felt.

And I want to feel it for the rest of my life.

Leading her up the path, I keep her close as the moon lights our way. I am nervous bringing her here to my place. Not just because it's the first time I have had a woman here. But because I am worried of what she might think. I do not live lavishly, and I wonder if it could be enough for her.

"Brett," she breathes as we stop just beyond the porch. "This is so beautiful. And totally not what I expected," she adds this in a wry tone, turning to grin up at me in the glowing light of the porch lights.

Turning to look over my home, I can't help but grin proudly. When I decided to come back home to Driftwood, I knew just the place I wanted to call home. Growing up here, I always wanted a spot on the mountain, close to the lodge I loved so much. Land on the mountain was not cheap so I figured it would always be nothing but a dream.

When I first won gold and endorsement deals started coming, I put all that money away. I knew I would come home to Driftwood when I was done competing. Once I retired, I bought the biggest plot of land on the mountain I could and built the place I had dreamed about for so long.

It's not a mansion. It's not high on the hill with the other elite of Driftwood. It's a cabin I designed and built. The very first place since I lost my grandfather that feels like home. To me it's the most beautiful spot in town. And sharing it with Brielle feels special.

Letting go of my hand, she walks up the wrap around porch. In the glow of the lights lining the porch, she looks stunning. Heading for the swing at the far end, she sits down and pushes herself gently. Glancing at me, she smirks and pats the empty spot beside her. I do not hesitate to join her.

"I take it back," she says as she turns to face me. "This place suits you. It's perfect. Give me a tour, Ace," she hums softly, tilting her head at the door.

Nodding, I take her hand and lead her inside. When we step inside, I find myself holding my breath. I want her to love it the way I do. Walking past me, keeping hold of my hand, she forgets about the tour. I let her wander around, not wanting to show off the big kitchen with the butcher block counters and touches of soft green. Instead of taking the lead, I follow her, and it feels as if I am seeing the place with brand new eyes.

Brielle comments on the thick beige rug in the front room, spread out by the floor-to-ceiling fireplace. It is framed by expansive windows, giving a beautiful view of the town below. Heading to those windows, she sighs as she stars out at the flickering lights of town, the gray skies blanketing everything in a soft glow.

"God it is so beautiful here," she whispers again, shaking her head.

Going to stand behind her, I cannot take my eyes off her. It is not the view that has me speechless. It is her. Seeing her in my place, seeing her love it the way I do—the way I hoped she would. I am more convinced than ever that she is the girl of my dreams—and I intend to do whatever it takes to prove I can be the man of her dreams.

"Tell your father you do not need to go home to find a fiancé. Tell him you have one," hearing this said out loud I realize how crazy it sounds. But I don't care. And I don't care that I am pretending to be her hero when really, I am taking advantage of her situation. Whatever it takes to get me the girl.

"Pretty sure he expects me to produce said fiancé at some point. Can't really do that if I am faking being.... oh...oh, no. No. No way, Ace."

"Now, did we not get past that when I made you come in my mouth tonight?"

Her little gasp as she turns to glare up at me makes my cock jerk. I step closer, backing her against the windows. Her breath picks up as her eyes darken, the pupils getting huge. And I know. I know that this turns her on as much as it does me. This dance we do. I thought her blowing me off was fun for her—thought it was the spoiled princess showing a cocky rich prick he could never have her.

Now I know better—I know she wants me as badly as I want her.

At last, I got past her walls and now I need to make sure to stay there. I spent months chasing her, flirting, laying all my cards out as I became increasingly obsessed with her. Until tonight I thought it was getting me nowhere. It was all self-preservation. Testing the meddle of another man who she thought would try to control her the way it sounds her father has.

Brielle is a beautiful, rich, powerful woman who could have any man she wants. But she does not trust herself or what she wants. All this cloak and dagger, all this dancing around the heat that sizzles between us was just her protecting herself. But I want to be the one to protect her—even if it means I play the bad guy for a little while.

"Stop it," she repeats the same words she said earlier, just before she let me make her come. Like then, she does not mean it. I would stop if she did. As my hand slips up her thigh, pushing aside the slit in her sexy dress, I can feel her body respond. Her breath catches as she stares up at me, her body trembling.

"Do you want me to stop, bunny? I don't think so," I whisper against her cheek as I press my lips there, breathing in her sweet scent. My hand slips up to her hip and I pull at her panties, snapping them to let them fall away.

"I don't.... I don't want you to. But I... oh!" she cries out as I yank at her thigh, dragging it over my hip as I slam her back against the window. My other hand slides up into her long, silky hair and I yank her head back.

"You know how badly I want you. Have wanted you since the day you came crashing down that hill. Let me have you, bunny. Let me take care of you, Brielle. Because I want to. I don't want anyone else to take care of you," I whisper the words against her lips as rage fills me at the very idea of someone else getting the privilege. I won't stand for it. I want to be the one to spoil her, to be there for her, the one she can trust and turn to.

Twisting, I notch my cock between her thighs and rock my hips. Her pussy is wet, soaking through my zipper. I growl and lift her against me, letting her rub her needy sex against my hard cock. I press my face against her neck, struggling to maintain control. I want to lose it, I want to rip her dress off and fuck her right here against this window, but I need her to ask for her. I need her to beg me for it, so I know she is in the same place I am.

Desperate and insatiable for one thing—one another.

"Tell your father he doesn't need to find you a fiancé. Be my plus one at all the holiday shindigs all the *Greta's* of Driftwood expect me at. We can help one another out, baby," I husk, dragging my lips up her throat slowly.

Brielle moans as she rocks against me, her tits crushed to my chest, her fingers tugging at my hair. When she pulls hard, I tilt my head back and meet her halfway for the kiss she seeks. Her tongue pushes into my mouth and I groan, my hands sliding beneath her ass to help her rock faster.

"Say yes, bunny," I grunt against her mouth, slipping my fingers between her thighs. Her slit is soaked, dripping against me as she whimpers, throwing her head back. "Be my date for the holidays. We can convince them all that we are crazy about each other," I smile against her mouth as I lick the sexy shape of her lips. It won't be hard for me to convince someone of how crazy I am about her.

"What if we can't fake it?" Brielle's voice is shaking, her hips twisting faster as she chases her orgasm.

"Oh bunny," I grunt, slamming my hips up so my stiff dick hits her swollen clit. "Do we need to fake it?"

Our eyes lock as she comes, shouting my name as I hold her close, watching the beauty of her climax wash over her. I will let her think this is all a sham, a pretense to protect us both this holiday season. As she curls against me and kisses me deep and hard, I know the answer she never gives me.

No, we won't have to fake it at all.

Chapter Six

Brielle

Boring has a color to it.

It is shiny and glittering but cold. It glistens in the light but in the darkness, it is empty. Those who have never seen a façade of happiness worn by a mask at a party might miss it. They might be intrigued by the glitz and glossiness but beneath that shine, there is nothing alluring at all.

Circling a glittering holiday event with a flute of expensive champagne, I bite back a smirk. Across the room, Brett is charming the host, none other than Grouchy Greta. When he showed up with me on his arm, it was obvious she was bothered. It should not have shocked her—we have been to three other of these sort of events since the one he hosted.

Being his plus one to these holiday events has been the best time of my life. Each event serves exactly two purposes for him: first, to donate more than all the rich folks who used to look down their noses at him, no matter the charity. Second, to make the rounds with me on his arm as his fiancé.

We have been to four holiday parties since his, and each one is more fun. Together we make the rounds, donate money or pricey items to the charities they claim to be concerned about, and piss off the stuffed shirts. We dance, drink, and have a damn good time together, all while we put on a show. Pretending we are madly in love and rushing to tie the knot.

"I will make the entire world believe you said yes to me, bunny," he swore that first night he took me home.

He had just given me a second orgasm, one of the most intense and intimate of my life, after taking me to his place. He heard all my father's demands and knew how lost I was after I was cut off. I do not care about the money all that much, really. To have my own father tell me nothing I have done was worthy of anything, that is what hurt.

Maybe I don't sit behind a desk creating software or designing tech. I always believed I was doing something more important. Leaving behind a legacy of doing for others, giving back, and seeking some sustainability.

"What if he does not believe it, Brett? What if my father tries to make me leave Driftwood?" my panic was obvious as we sat by his fireplace that night, talking about this plan of his—one I was way too agreeable with.

Fake being his fiancé for a few months? I can do that.

"Oh, bunny, he will have no doubt that we're going to get married. And I won't ever let him or anyone else make you do anything. Do you trust me?"

There was no hesitation as he asked that, gazing down at me with honesty in his beautiful golden eyes. *"Yes, Brett, I trust you."*

Tonight, he said to enjoy the pricey champagne and hors d'oeuvres as he makes Greta regret being a bitch before. His way of making her pay is to brag about our engagement and how extravagant our wedding will be. I laugh as I hear him telling her about a winter wedding with a fairytale carriage and diamond glass slippers.

When he first he brought up our nuptials it was a grand tale about a destination wedding in Ireland. Then he said we would be going to a secluded island with just the most important people in our lives. This story he is telling now, this is my favorite so far. I laugh when Greta shoots a glare my way as he mentions dress fittings in Paris.

"Sweetheart, stop boring these people," I tease as I slide up to his side, catching my breath when he turns his attention on me, pulling me close.

Brett grins at me and for a moment, it feels as if this whole thing is real. As if I really am his fiancé, not just a fake using him to get my father off my back. Lowering his head, he brushes his nose against mine and presses a featherlight kiss to my lips. Like any time he touches me, my world loses focus and becomes all about sensation.

Since he took me home that night, I have not left his place. He has also not touched me the way he did that night. He gave up his bed for me and sleeps on the couch even though *I wanted* to share a bed. Lennon knows what is going on and thinks it's the best thing that could have happened—she has been pushing me to give him a real shot since we met.

It may have taken me a bit longer to agree, but I am all for giving him a shot. Now that we have been pretending to be crazy about one another, I finally realize I really am crazy about him. He makes me laugh, he is smart, kind, and he is more genuine than I ever gave him credit for.

We have been faking this for a while—now I want the real thing.

"You look stunning tonight, bunny," he purrs softly against my ear as we spin away from the crowd, dancing without music. "Did I tell you how good you looked yet?"

Nodding, I tilt back, gazing up at him in the glittering light. Greta went all out for her soiree, with twinkling lights hanging from the ceiling and all size of glowing golden snowflakes filling the room. Brett looks delicious in a fitted suit jacket, sneakers, and a plain tee. Somehow, he makes everything look good. Noticing our hostess watching us, I know I am not the only one who thinks so, either.

"You did. After all, you did choose this dress tonight," I remind him that he gifted me this silky black satin dress earlier. He announced tonight was Greta's annual charity ball and we had to go. It was his idea of softening the blow by gifting me this stunning dress and a pair of Manolo's to match.

His eyes flare as we move further away from the crowd. I wonder if he remembers how I thanked him for the dress. Standing in front of the stunning fireplace in the front room of his cabin, I dropped the robe I had on to slide the dress on. I took my time, so he got a good look at what was beneath all this silky satin. Maybe I hoped he would forget about coming here tonight and rip the dress off me, but no dice.

"Well, it suits you. I enjoyed watching you put it on," he teases, voice rough against my ear, "but I will enjoy watching you take it off more, bunny," he pulls my head back gently, our eyes meeting as I feel the cool night air on my skin.

Realizing he has danced us right out of the room and onto a balcony, I want to laugh. He is always sneaking me off somewhere when we come to these things. That first night he took me to the stairwell to do filthy things to me. Two nights ago, we snuck off to the roof of one of his rich friends' downtown lofts to watch the snow fall, and we made out like teenagers.

"Is that so? Am I putting on a show for you later then, ace?" I tease as he lifts me atop the wide balcony, stepping between my legs.

"Just you existing is a show for me, bunny," he whispers, his breath curling in the frigid air, "I wish you realized how absolutely enchanted I am by you. You are the most beautiful thing I have ever set sight on."

Wanting the same thing, we move at the same time. I bend as he lifts, our mouths meeting in a frenzied kiss. His hands slide over my bare back, burning my skin as he pulls at the tiny straps of the dress. I pull back, letting the top of the silk fall away, baring myself to him.

"You look at me as if you mean that," I tell him breathlessly and he pauses the path of kisses he was working down my throat.

He pulls back, tilting his head, his golden eyes glittering in the darkness. Reaching a hand up, he cradles my face, tilting my head back. His thumb rubs at my swollen bottom lip and I nip at it. My pulse is thrumming beneath his heavy gaze, and I feel my heart galloping in my chest.

"Because I do mean it. Do you know how impossible it is to have you in my bed and...and not do the things I have dreamt of doing to you?"

"Why...why haven't you then?" I cut him off when he starts to go on.

Brett lowers his head, so his words are breathed against my mouth. "Because, Bunny, you have not asked me to. Is this you asking me?"

"Yes," I pant the word, clutching at his jacket to tug him closer. "Yes, I am asking. Don't make me spend another night alone in bed, Brett."

As if my words seal the deal, things shift between us, and I know they won't ever go back again. Never again can I pretend he is just a rich playboy I want nothing to do with. I won't be able to blow off his flirtations the way I did before. I no longer want to protect myself from him.

However he may ruin me, I want it.

Because I know this pleasure will be worth whatever it may cost me down the road. Brett makes me feel things I only read about in books before—in fantasies about perfect men who know how to touch you, know what filthy things to say to you, and who stick around after they do their worst.

"Let's go."

Almost giggling as he rushes to fix the straps on my dress, I let him pull me from the ledge. We stumble inside, tangled up and laughing still. All eyes fall on us, my dress hanging wrong, his jacket a mess from my hands, and my makeup smudged. Neither of us seem to care as they whisper their dislike for our flagrant dalliances. We want them to buy that we're crazy about each other after all, don't we?

Lovers rushing off to climb in bed ought to do the trick.

Once he loads me in the back of his waiting car, I do not waste another moment. I climb into his lap, winding my arms around his neck as I fit close. I cover his mouth with mine, tasting champagne and chocolates. I moan as his tongue comes out, licking at my mouth before our tongues tangle.

Fingers tangling in his thick hair, I kiss him greedily as his hands slide up my back. He pulls at the thin straps of the dress again and I let it fall. His mouth tears from mine, moving down my throat, across my shoulders, sending heat swirling through me like a snowstorm.

"So soft, bunny," his raspy voice sends a shudder through me as he kisses at my breasts, his hands palming the aching flesh. His head tips back, eyes locking on mine as he flicks at my peaked nipple with his thumb. I cry out and the grin he rewards me with is so sexy, I shudder.

With his eyes still holding mine, he dips lower, flicking his tongue around my nipple. I gasp, my fingers tangling in his hair as I arc to his mouth. He sucks at my breast, his teeth scraping at my nipple, sending jolts of pleasure to my sex. I twist my hips against him, chasing the pleasure that pounds through me as he suckles and bites at my tender flesh.

"Brett, please...please, I need " my moan echoes in the small confines of the car, sounding needy and desperate to my own ears.

Head falling back, I rock on his lap, forgetting where we are and the driver in the front. All I care about is the pleasure he always gives me. It's more than simple orgasms. When he holds me, when he whispers in my ear and tells me how beautiful I am, how much he needs me, it's a lot more than pleasure. It's a connection unlike any I have felt with anyone else before.

Reaching between us, I fumble with the zipper on his slacks. He grunts something about me waiting. About doing this right. I am done waiting and if we both get what we need so badly, how can it be wrong? I slide backwards until I am kneeling before him, my hand closing around his thick dick. It's hard and heavy, velvet pulsing in my hand.

"Bunny, get back up here," he growls, smirking at me as I push his knees open to fit between them.

"Got me down on my knees.... can't you think of something I could do for you, Ace?" I rasp, trailing my finger up and down his shaft slowly.

"Open your mouth," he grunts as his eyes darken, his jaw ticking.

Heat simmers in his eyes as his hands come to the back of my head. My mouth pops open and I sense how much he loves that I obey him. Slowly, he draws me closer, and I dart my tongue out to lick the tip of him. Humming at the saltines of him, I take him past my lips and deep into my mouth.

"Ah, Christ," he growls, head falling back as my tongue traces the veiny length of him.

Seeing someone as controlled and sexy as Brett start to lose control is the hottest thing I have ever seen. Knowing I am the one undoing that control turns me on like nothing else ever has. I am soaked between my thighs as I start to suck him deeper, deeper, swirling my tongue as I bob my head.

"God, that's it. Fuck, I want to come down your throat, bunny. Can you swallow me down, baby? Will you take me in that pretty mouth?"

Nodding, I suck harder, cheeks hallowing out as I turn wild. I want to taste him as he comes. I want to make it so good for him. I wrap my hand around the base of him, pumping in rhythm as I suck him deeper, feeling him start to jerk in my mouth. He growls as his fingers tangle in my hair, holding me still as he comes.

Brett lets out a carnal growl, sending a shockwave of pleasure through me. As he comes, spurting down my throat, a small orgasm winds through me. While he holds me still, pumping his hips slightly, I moan and come too, my thighs rubbing to work out the small tremors of my climax.

"Ah, hell, bunny. Come here, baby," he coos roughly.

Scooping me up, he settles me on his lap as we catch our breath. It's then I realize we are outside his place and have been for some time. Without a word, he opens the back door and steps out, still clutching me to him. I don't let go as he rushes up the long walk and stomps up the front porch. When he throws open the front door then kicks it behind him, I smile against his neck.

As his footsteps sound on the hardwood floors, a shiver runs through me. I sense where he is headed. I clutch him closer, my limbs tight at his hips and shoulders. I gasp softly when I feel him lie me back on his bed, but he doesn't move away. He fits his body against mine, pinning me beneath him.

"Eager tonight, Ace?" I tease, brushing my lips at his ear.

"Oh, yes. Eager for you to realize what I have known for months."

Lying back as he pulls away slightly, I gaze up into his shimmering eyes. I know just what he means but I want to hear him say it. "And what do you want me to realize?"

"Nothing needs faking between us, does it, bunny?"

Chapter Seven

Brett

Looking at my future is the most powerful moment of my life.

Brielle is spread out in my bed, waiting for me to take her. It's been two weeks since I first brought her home and asked her to be my date to half a dozen holiday parties. Taking her to those parties has been the most fun I have ever had. We go and have a good time and have made it a game to donate more money than anyone else to whatever charities the party is for.

Never once have we had to fake it. No one doubted for one moment that we are a couple. That we are nuts over each other. It's obvious when you see us together. For a while she was able to fool herself that there was nothing between us, but I knew better. It was there that first day on the mountain.

"Take off that dress for me," I rasp as I stand at the edge of the bed, watching her sit up, her slinky silk dress slipping off her shoulders.

This sexy dress was one I chose for her. I picked that silky number that cost a fortune and the flashy heels I plan to leave on while I fuck her. Going to that party tonight I wanted her to turn heads. Those haughty broads were jealous of how stunning she looked and every rich suit there was pissed she was coming home with me.

No one will ever doubt again—her included—that she is my fiancé.

Sitting forward, she does a shimmy to let the dress fall to her waist. Her full, pear-shaped tits are bare, the pink nipples stiff, still wet from my mouth suckling at them earlier. Reaching out, I tug at the left one, her breathy gasp making my dick jerk in my slacks.

"Lie back. I want to see you bare," I demand as I step back to watch.

As she falls back against the bed, the dress bunches at her hips. I grasp it and gently work it down her thighs and off. Her body is perfection. Wide hips and thick thighs, her right thigh has a strawberry-colored birthmark shaped like a heart. Dropping to kneel between her thighs, I dip my head to kiss at the mark, lavishing it with my lips.

Her head goes back, her eyes closing, and I sigh against her skin. It's taken us some time to get here, but here we are. Not just here in my bed. Here together where I always believed we belonged. With her trusting me. Giving in to me and what we feel for one another.

Kissing her other thigh, I lift it atop my shoulder, smiling when her hips twist. I can smell how turned on she is. Her pussy tastes like strawberries and cream, as if that sexy birthmark is a hot clue. Kissing gently at the soft swell of her stomach and the dips and curves of her wide waist, I leave no part of her untouched.

My hands slide up the back of her calves, smoothing over her creamy thighs. I spread them apart, dipping my head to nuzzle my nose against her mound. Flicking my tongue out, I lick her slit wide open and she moans deep and throaty, her back arching off the bed. Moving a hand up, I push her pelvis back down as my lips close around her clit.

"Holy Jesus," she moans loudly, hands coming to cup the back of my head. Her fingers thread in my hair, tugging, twisting, her hips circling against my tongue.

I eat at her slowly, sucking at her nub until her thighs begin to quake. I pull back then, licking at her dripping center, suckling noisily at her juices. Now she bucks her hips, shoving her pussy at my mouth. Lifting my head, I grin up at her from between her thighs.

"Be still, bunny. Let me savor you the way I want to," I tell her, scrapping my teeth across her pulsing clit again.

Brielle shouts, holding my mouth to her. My lips close at her clit as my fingers join the party. I curl two inside of her, the tips of my fingers finding her rough patch of nerves, rubbing slowly. I watch her skin glow in the dim moonlight as she begins to pant.

"Oh! Brett....baby, I'm coming!"

As she comes, I rub harder at her g-spot, suckling at her juice as she floods my mouth. One orgasm turns to another as I pump my fingers faster, her pussy spasming tight. Flicking my eyes up, I watch her palm her tits as she goes through the aftershocks of her climax.

While she is still quivering, I move over her, dropping my clothes as I kneel between her legs. My cock is stiff, pointing at her hungrily. Dripping excitement from the tip, it's throbbing as I wrap a hand around it, pumping slowly. I swipe my fingers through her messy folds, grunting as I rub her cum on my dick, lubing my length up.

"Christ watching you come is like finding a religion. When I get inside you, bunny," I rasp, watching her eyes glitter in the dark, "it will be finding heaven. And I won't ever want to come back out," I admit roughly.

"Come here, baby," she coos, reaching for me. "Come here, I want us both to find heaven."

Letting her pull me atop her, I grit my teeth as her soft thighs and softer tits welcome my hardness. It is heaven. No gold, no trophy, no amount of money or success could ever compare to just having her beneath me. Pushing up on fists balanced beside her hips, I gaze down at her.

Words cannot come close to what I feel in this moment. Wanting her for so long has left me feeling half empty. Only owning her will make me whole again. Will fill up that part of me that has craved her. That has needed her.

That aching part that has loved her.

"Nothing between us," I whisper shakily as I line myself up, rubbing my stiff shaft between her sticky sex. "Ever. I want to feel every pulse of you when you come with me inside you. I want every drop of my cum deep inside you, bunny," I declare roughly, slowly pushing the tip inside.

"Brett...please...." she moans the words, nodding in agreement.

"Told you I had another reason for calling you bunny," I tease with a smirk as I press my mouth to her ear, "because we will be fucking like bunnies, Brielle. And making babies like rabbits."

Slamming home, a shudder overcomes me as her pussy closes painfully tight around my shaft. A small orgasm ripples up my cock as she shakes, clawing at my back. Lifting slightly, I take her mouth as I start to move. Her tongue strokes mine as I fuck her, darting forward, back, keeping rhythm.

Wrapping her long hair around my fist, I pull back, wanting to watch her as I claim her. Her eyes glisten in the darkness and I know she is feeling what I am. Pressing my forehead to hers, I whisper her name again and again. I tell her how good she feels wrapped around me. How soft she is pressed close as she clutches me tight. I tell her how beautiful she is each time she edges another orgasm. How adorable she pouts when I refuse her, pulling out and pinching her clit to tease her.

"You want to come, bunny? Ask me for it. I need to know you need it. I need to know it's burning you up. Beg me for it, bunny. Beg me to let you come on my cock."

Brielle shouts, clawing at my back and sending a shower of pleasure burning right to my balls. I pound her faster, harder, then pull out all the way. I watch her pretty pussy clench, seeking the stretch of my cock filling her. I plunge balls deep and bend my head, suckling at her throat, biting at her nipples, slamming deeper and deeper inside her.

"Ah, let me come! Please! I need to baby, please.... oh yes! Oh god!"

My hips throw violently as she gives me what I want. I bend her thighs backwards, pumping faster, both of us sticky with sweat. I spit on her pussy and rub at her clit, feeling her coming so hard she pushes me out of her tight cunt. I push back in and pound faster, racing to come with her, to come inside of her, to fill her up with my cum.

"That's it. That's it, bunny. That's my girl, fuck, choke me with that greedy pussy. Fuck, I'm....ah, yes, that's it. I'm coming, bunny."

"Come inside me," she moans as she pulls me close, panting against my ear, "please, I want to feel you come, baby."

Never once did I plan to pull out, but her begging for it shoves me over the precipice. I lean in, taking her filthy talking mouth in a brutal kiss. I pump a few times before I growl as her tightness goes even tighter, sucking me deeper. I pant against her mouth, chanting her name as I come hard.

Rolling off her, I catch my breath as I pull her across my chest. We're a mess, the sheets are twisted up at our feet, and our clothes lie in a heap at the end of the bed. Usually, a mess would stress me out, but I don't care.

There is nothing I would change about this moment.

Nothing at all I would change about this night or how we got here.

Brielle needs me right now, but I need to make sure that lasts. I need to do whatever it takes to make certain she always needs me. Not just to be her hero or be her fake Holi-date. I need to convince her that she will always need me and what I can do for her. All that I can make her feel. Everything that I can give her that no one else can.

How do I convince a girl who once had everything that I can give her anything she cannot get herself?

Chapter Eight

Brielle

Watching women flirt with my date makes me horny.

It makes me hot because while they bat their pretty lashes at him and sashay their perfect asses by, he never takes his eyes off me. No matter who comes to take us away from one another—women wanting his attention or men wanting his money—we find our way right back to each other.

Tonight, is the eighth—yes, I have kept count—fancy schmancy function we have been to since this fake-a-date thing began. Only he has spent every moment between doing his very best to convince me, and anyone else who wants to listen, that there is nothing fake about us.

Every single time he calls me his fiancé and looks at me with that possessive heat in his eyes, my lady parts swoon. By the end of one of these nights out, where he says loud and proud how hot his lady is and how he can't wait to get married and give me babies, my poor lady business is a mess.

And each night once he gets me home, he proves that he means all that talk. Sometimes we barely get inside his house before he has me bent over or spread out, fucking me like he can't wait to a second longer to put his mark on me. Not that his beard, his teeth, or his rough hands have not left plenty of marks on me.

Glancing at myself in a floor-to-ceiling mirror, I flush. I can see love bites sneaking out of my ruby red dress. Beneath the dress is worse, his teeth marks at my nipple, his beard rash at my thighs downright salacious. And I love seeing it and love that others see it too.

They know what I am just accepting—I am his, nothing fake about it.

"Come here, bunny," he calls to me, tilting his head as he grins. He knows how much I love that little pet name, even more now that he told me just why he calls me that.

"We will be fucking like bunnies, Brielle. And making babies like rabbits."

Just recalling his sex voice as he whispered that in my ear makes me hot. I rub my thighs together as he crosses the room towards me, downing my champagne. Our eyes meet and I laugh. He knows exactly what I was thinking about. He loves to tease me about how dirty we talk in bed and how shy I get about it later.

"Fuck me! Deeper, baby! I want to feel you come inside me."

Laughing as he moves close, nuzzling his face against my throat, I lace my arms at his neck. Just this afternoon we were at his place, setting up a Christmas tree. I no sooner got the star on the top and he had his face buried beneath my skirt. He pressed me against the huge windows after he stripped me bare, fucking me deep and hard until I came three times.

This man is the best fake boyfriend I have ever had.

"Stop thinking dirty things, bunny," he hums against my throat. "Or I will just have to find a way to give you those dirty things. You know I cannot say no to you, baby," he reminds me, and I smile as I snuggle against him.

This is true. Besides spoiling me with new dresses for each of these parties we have attended, and matching shoes and purses if he feels lavish, he has given me everything I ask for. One night I was craving chocolate chip cookies. We drove to town where I expected to buy some. No, he never does anything simple.

Brett bought all the best ingredients, and we went back home, where he pulled out his grandmother's fragile recipe. He turned on Christmas carols and we sang and cooked the best chocolate chip cookies I have ever had. It was not just about cookies though—he created one of the most significant nights of my life.

"Promises, promises,' I tease, kissing his jaw as I tilt his head back.

God, he is a beautiful man. How did I ever pretend I was not smitten? From that day he waited at the bottom of the slope, my handsome savior, I put up a barrier. Ones he has broken past one by one.

At night, we talk about everything I never talked about with anyone else. Even things I never shared with Lennon or Quinn. He tells me about Shea Ski Lodge and how much it means to him. How much his grandfather meant to him. And I tell him how much I miss my mom even though I barely remember her.

"I wish...I wish I could just remember her perfume or what her voice sounded like. All I have are photos. Glimpses of moments. Father won't talk about her and my brother...he was so close to her it's too hard on him."

"I can give you so much," he had whispered to me as I admitted this painful truth to him. *"Except the thing you want the most. It kills me to see you hurt. I am sure she would be so proud of you. Proud of the woman you grew up to be."*

It was just a few nights back when we laid by the fireplace, bare as the day we were born with snow falling from gray skies, I knew he was not the man I believed him to be. He was not some playboy—he had just played one on TV. And just to showcase the lodge, to do right by his grandfather.

Brett Shea is possibly the best man I had ever met. He hosted that charity the night he took me home for the right reasons. Well, he claims he hosted it to lure me to the lodge, knowing damn well I could not help myself. And all these fake dates we go out on, to all the most important holiday events, are just a way for him to give back because he can.

"I keep my promises to you, bunny," he purrs, pressing a wet kiss to my throat as his fingers trace down the neckline of my dress.

"Brett, baby, don't tease me," I whimper, tilting my head back as he walks me out of the room. Always finding a way to escape, this one.

"Have I broken one promise yet? Tell me one," he taunts me as he walks me onto a terrace.

It's chilly with flurries sailing down slowly in big, thick flakes. Skies overhead are gray but dotted with stars here and there. A glance back at the mountainside shows smokestacks and pricks of lights where the lumberjacks of Driftwood make their homes. It's like a scene right out of a snow globe.

"Make me a promise now," I whisper as I spin in his arms, staring up at the beautiful view. "This moment right here...capture it for me somehow. And the first moments we danced that night at the lodge. Our night making cookies. Can you capture those for me? Because I don't want to lose them."

Emotion makes my voice tremble and I realize I am scared. I am trembling not from the cold at all. I am terrified. I weighed what I was worth for so long by what I could give. What pricey gifts I gave for special occasions or the places I flew off to when we wanted to get away. The wealth I had grown up with was all I had going for me. It was how I mattered in the world—because I tried to do good with it.

Before I never considered my worth as a person. Was I kind? Was I caring? Did I make people laugh? Did I make people happier for knowing me? All these things, I had never had to think about because I could donate to a shelter or a cause to feel good and kind. If someone was sad, I could cheer them up by going to Disneyland and shutting it down for us. None of that counts towards who or what I am as a person. Not really.

I am scared that Brett knows all of that. That he wants me now because I am shiny and pretty enough to show off at these holiday parties. I want to believe that he has been feeling what I have, that there is really nothing fake about this. But I can't let myself believe anything. I am afraid he wants to fake this just long enough to get through the season. After that I will be left out in the cold.

I am afraid that once the new year hits, I will have lost him along with everything else.

"Bunny, talk to me," he husks as his warm hands frame my face. "What is going on in that beautiful brain of yours? You look terrified."

Blinking up at him as snow coats his dark jacket and dots his dark hair, I realize tears blur my vision. And he is still beautiful. I try to hide my tears, but his face darkens once he sees them. He dips his head, brushing his lips on my cheeks, kissing the tears away.

"Bunny," his voice is so gentle my tears just fall faster. "What is it?"

"I...I thought I was a good person. Now I think...since my father cut me off, what have I done? Let you spoil me and take care of me. All I have ever done is spend someone else's money. I have never done something worthwhile. I am starting to think I am just as worthless as he said I am."

A muffled sound vibrates from deep in his chest. The twinkling lights shine in his dark eyes as they flare hot. Not with the heat I am so accustomed to. But with anger. No, with rage. He told me how little he thinks of my father after what happened, but I don't think I fully understood until this moment.

"He will regret the day he spoke to you that way. How could you ever doubt you are good? You are...Brielle, you are the sweetest, most honest, brightest, and most giving person I have ever met. You did not traipse across the globe to take selfies to post to Instagram. You were in the trenches, saving homes, protesting injustices and cruelties, and you have saved lives."

"But did I do it for them...or did I do all of that for me?"

"Someone might say it matters, but I don't think it does. What has any of us done that is not a little self-serving?"

"What have you ever done that was self-serving?"

"You, bunny. Pretending at these parties, so the world, most importantly your piece of shit father, see that we're headed down the aisle. That is one of the most self-serving things I have ever done, Brielle."

Fear pulses through my veins like a sickness. I stumble, falling back against the stone pillars surrounding the terrace. We're lit by twinkling lights, but it feels darker, colder, as I stare at him. I am afraid to ask what he means. But as is often the case with Brett North, he does not make me wait.

"Because I did it for me. Because I want you. I would lie, cheat, steal, and lie again to have you. I would do anything for you. Don't you see that?"

"Why? What is so special about me? What have I done to deserve..."

"Bunny, I told you.... all you have to do is exist," his voice trembles as he presses close, pinning me to the pillar.

Gazing up at him, I make a decision. Maybe I am not worthy of him or of anyone. Father might be right that I have done nothing worth mention in my twenty-five years. But with him, right now at least, that does not matter.

I decide to fake it as long as he will let me.

"Keep your promise," I rasp, lifting my leg until he hooks his hand beneath my knee.

"What promise...oh, bunny," his voice turns hot as he sees the intent swirling my eyes.

Reaching between us, I swiftly unzip his slacks and slide my hand inside. He is hot, despite the frigid temperatures, his shaft thick and hard in my hand. I push at his boxers and pants until he springs free. Pumping him slowly, I focus on his eyes. His eyes always tell me what I need to know. If he needs harder, slower, or faster and wetter.

Spitting on my hand, I laugh when he groans, and his head falls back. I work him harder, faster, panting as I watch him give in. He always gives in spoils me by giving me what I need. And right now, I need him.

"Please, Ace," I taunt, rubbing my thumb at his swollen tip.

"Quiet. Don't make a sound. We don't want someone to interrupt."

Nodding, I pointedly seal my lips, but he just laughs. We both know once he gets me going, I won't be quiet. I can't be once he starts touching me. Once he fills me and stretches me, fitting me to him in that way that makes me believe I was meant just for him, I can't stay quiet. And he is lying—he does not care if we get caught. In fact, I think the risk turns him on.

Brett steps back, his foot kicking at mine to force my stance to widen, His hand passes by mine that still strokes him, pushing my panties to the side. He hisses when he finds me wet, his rough fingers rubbing at me. I don't need him to get me ready. I have been ready since that blonde was flirting with him earlier, but he had eyes only for me.

Bringing his wet fingers to my mouth, he coats my lips in my own arousal. Groaning when I stick my tongue out, he bends and licks at my sticky lips then kisses me hard. Gripping my hip, he tilts me slightly. When he thrusts, sinking deep in one stroke, his mouth swallows my moan.

"Hush, bunny," he reminds me as he flips his hand between my legs, rubbing at my clit. "Be good for me. Let me fuck you, baby. I ought to come deep in this pussy before you get off. Teach you to doubt your worth for even a moment. Fuck. Don't you come, bunny. Let me get...fuck, that's it, let that pussy choke my cock. God, I love being inside you, baby."

For telling me to be quiet, his filthy words are echoing loudly. I laugh when he glances back towards the party cautiously. If someone heard, they could find us any moment. He thrusts faster, pounding into me as he rubs faster, harder at my clit, his mouth sealed to mine.

"Come, bunny," he grunts, fingers digging into my hip as he thrusts harder, lifting me off my feet with the force. "Come on my cock so I can fill this pretty pussy with my cum. Want you walking out of here dripping me out of you. Ah, fuck, that's it bunny."

I clutch at his shoulders as I throw my head back, screaming silently into the dark skies. I come so hard when I blink, I swear I seen lighting the skies. I collapse against him as he throws his hips a few times before he lifts me by the back of my thighs, forcing my limbs to close around him.

"I'm coming," he whispers against my mouth, panting as he jerks inside me, the moment so hot, so intense, we just stare into one another's eyes.

We catch our breath as the moment goes still. I whisper to him that I want him to capture this moment for me too. He chuckles and tells me he will find an X-rated artist to get it done for me. And as he kisses me, I wonder for a moment if he might mean it.

"Let's go home, bunny," he coos as he fixes my dress and tucks my panties back in place.

"Yeah, Ace, let's go home."

He leads me through the crowd inside and I just know they all have every idea what we just did outside. But neither of us care. We come to these things to prove to people who talk that we plan to get married. That he is the future I have chosen for myself. All so my father cannot force me to make an impossible choice.

Cuddled together on the way back home, I wonder if I could make a choice if he tried to force me to. Could I ever choose anyone else but Brett? When he carries me inside and to bed, where he spends the rest of the night proving just what I am worth to him, I know my answer.

How could I ever choose anyone but that man I love?

Chapter Nine

Brett

Christmas this year could be the last I spend single.

Not that I consider myself single. If you're asking me, I have been taken since Brielle slid down the mountain side to land at my feet. I was taken the moment those glittering blue eyes gazed up at me. And when she mouthed off to me and told me to get lost, I knew she was the girl for me.

"Diamond....or some other precious stone? You girls know her best."

Showing Brielle's besties the drawings Rian Thorne has done, I ask for their input. Whatever they tell me is right for her, I will trust. They know her better than anyone else. Even though as of late, we have learned plenty about one another. That is why once they choose a ring, I am not surprised because it is my favorite and one, I hoped they would approve of.

A tear shaped pink diamond in a rose gold band crowned by sparkling diamonds, it is a beautiful design. The stones are naturally sourced, which I know will matter to her, and roughly cut. They sparkle just enough to catch the eye without being obnoxious and I cannot wait to see it on her hand.

"Really doing it then, Ace?" Lennon quips as I ask Rian to have it done up and ready to go by Christmas next week.

"Oh yes. I would have asked her the day she came crashing down that slope if I thought she would have said yes. Now I might have a shot at getting a yes. If not, I will keep at it until I win a yes from her."

"Who knows with Brielle, girl may have said yes that day if you asked right," Quinn teases with a chuckle before Lennon joins in.

They may be laughing about it, but I have thought of this moment for months. I want it to be perfect. But I have almost blurted it out and asked half a dozen times since she started staying at my place. Having her there is so right and I don't want her to find an excuse to leave.

Lennon told us both she could come back to their place at any time, but I know she wants her to stay with me too. Not because she does not want her best friend back as a roomie. But because she knows how crazy I am about her. How willing I am to take care of her and provide all she could ever need. But we all know those demands her father made of her still weigh on her.

Brielle spent most of her life trying to rid her guilt over being wealthy. Of having an entitled existence. Going to foreign countries to build wells and homes, protesting in the streets of Asia and Africa, and spending fortunes on donations did little to fill the emptiness her family carved inside her.

"A holiday proposal. It is so romantic. Brielle eats up romance like buttery scones," Lennon gushes, clutching her fists over her heart as she flutters her eyes at me playfully.

"Could have fooled me," I say with a laugh, "I tried to romance her for months before everything with her father. Part of me thinks..." trailing off, I shake my head because I don't genuinely believe those thoughts. I do not believe that she has stayed with me these past weeks because she felt obligated. Nothing that has happened between us is out of obligation.

"No, our girl loves romance and fluffy shit," Quinn states.

Good thing because my proposal is going to be fluffy. Making her friends promise to be there on Christmas, I head to Landon Holm's workshop to check how our project is coming. His door stands open, so I start to head in. Before I duck my head in to call hello, I hear it. I hear the rhythmic thud of a worktable slamming against the wall. I hear breathy moans. I start to back away when I hear his guttural growl.

"Good girl, songbird. Such a good girl for me, that's it."

His filthy words make me cringe and I slowly back up, hoping he does not realize I just caught him and his old lady hooking up. To be fair, it's not uncommon that someone catches the two of them. His wife Lilli is a romance author and uses her husband for plenty of material. At least, I have been told.

Just as I think I am home free, the door swings wide open. I am frozen on the spot. The air thickens as I lock eyes with Landon Holms. He is a huge man who is good with an axe. Catching him post coitus with his wife is not a good look. But he smirks and jerks his head to invite me in as Lilli giggles and sneaks to the front office where I think she has plenty to write about.

"Bro, I did not mean to interrupt," I put my hands up and I stay on my side of the threshold. "I came to talk...I barely heard anything. I mean, I certainly did not see anything," I rush the words out, backing up when he makes a menacing move forward.

"Calm down, Shea," he tells me, chuckling as he runs his hands through his mussed hair. "It ain't the first time and it won't be the last we got caught with our asses out. Come on, let me show you what I did for you."

Sighing in relief, I follow him inside the long, wide space. His workshop is a new space for him. Used to be he would work up on the mountain, at his cabin, whenever he wanted to create something. Now he takes holiday orders for one-of-a-kind gifts, so he needed the room. I whistle as I look at the space with brand new woodworking equipment and several beautiful pieces done and waiting to go to new homes.

"Wow, what I asked for must have been easy breezy compared to some of this stuff. Landon, this stuff is amazing," I praise him, going to inspect a beautiful armoire that sits waiting for delivery with a big bow on top.

"Well really, it was some challenging work with the details you wanted. Not that I do not love a challenge. Just ask my songbird," he mentions his wife with a smile, his eyes flying to his office where Fleetwood Mac thumps.

"I am excited to see them. I just know my bunny is going to love them."

Following him to a table, I stop as I see what is spread out atop it. My breath catches in my lungs as my heartbeat slows. I reach out to touch the closest one and my pulse picks back up. It is cookies and snowflakes with a mountain view. The one next to it is a ski slope and a clumsy bunny. But my favorite has the lodge and two people dancing.

Wooden snow globes with no fake snow or fake memories—pieces of walnut and maple, carved with our memories and lit twinkling lights lighting up the moments my bunny asked me to capture for us. There are others, ones of us tangled together on a wintery terrace, or cuddled by a fire. All moments I could never forget—and ones I clearly gave Landon enough detail to carve the most beautiful gift I could give her.

"Jesus, Landon," I mutter as I pick each one up, turning them, looking at each detail. "Whatever I agreed to pay, triple it. I mean it. These are...were you there watching us, you sneaky fuck?" I laugh as I ask, just to hide the emotion that is making it hard to speak at all.

"No, I think just maybe, someone captured things so well, I had a chance to bring them to life. Glad I got it right for you."

"Got it right? Christ, these are...they are like reliving each moment. I mean it," I give him a hard look, "what did we agree on? Whatever it is, I am tripling it. This is beyond...this is far more than I expected, bro. Wow. I just...all I can really say is wow. I am blown away. Thank you. My bunny is going to...this is going to make her holiday, I hope. Thank you, Landon."

My lumberjack friend waves it off, but I can tell he is pleased with his work. And he should be. I wanted snow globes for her, to show her how each of these moments were special to me like they were to her. They could be something she could hold on to if ever she doubted how I feel for her.

These show...at least, *I hope* they show, how much I love her.

Landon tells me they will be ready to go after the finishing touches by Christmas day. I insist on him tripling the payment we agreed on, even though we both know he does not need the money. But I want him to have it because he earned every penny. I tell him I will be bragging to all the rich pricks at Shea Lodge how amazing he is so they can stuff his pockets more.

With my tasks done for the day, I head back home. Just knowing that Brielle is at home waiting for me fills me with a joy I never thought I would feel. My grandparents loved each other but it was very private for them. He was different after he lost her. When he got sick, he seemed happier—he said he was on his trip back to her so there was nothing to be sad about.

If I can have that kind of love, I will hold on to it with both hands. Just the way they did. What we have is just for us too. Yes, we've been parading it at these parties but that's just for show. That is just to shut up the women who chase me to get to my wallet and to get her father off her back.

"*When you look at me,*" she had whispered to me one night as we laid in bed sipping wine and wasting the night away together. "*I feel as if...it sounds so cliché but, I mean it. I feel sometimes when you look at me, as if my life makes sense. As if the way you look at me makes everything make sense.*"

It hardly sounded cliched to me. We were made for one another, the two of us. My sweet, sexy, sassy bunny is like the other half of me. Now I have to convince her I am the other half of her, too. That she does not need her father or her brother to give her a thing. To reinstate her black cards or dole out an allowance to her. Brielle will never need them while I am in her life.

I can give her all they ever could and more—because at least I can give her the love that she wants so badly.

Pulling down the long drive leading to my cabin, my senses go on alert. It is dark out, and I spent most of the day in town. Fresh snow fell all morning. There should be no tracks because mine from leaving should be covered. Rolling out in front of me are wide, deep truck tracks. I hit the gas and shoot down the drive, whipping my jeep around in front of the house and jumping out.

Rushing up the steps, I throw the door open, reaching for the shotgun hidden in a panel beside the door. It is bear country here, I have weapons stashed all over the house for safety. When I find who caused those tracks though, I know none of these weapons will be any good on them.

"Bunny," I call out to my woman when I see two men flanking her, the younger man looking to be her twin. "Come here."

Without hesitation, she rushes to me, her little body slamming against mine. I ought to use that shotgun on those pricks anyway. I kiss the top of her head as she clings to me. Whatever they want, whatever they have said to her, it has her trembling. I slam the door behind me and calm myself before I greet our visitors.

"Mr. North, I wish I had known you were coming to town. Caleb," I toss a less curt greeting at her brother, but her father deserves all my ire.

"At least I know he does his homework," her father sneers at us as he says this to her brother, as if we're not there to hear him. "So do we. I figured my daughter had found someone to take care of her. But your services are no longer required, Mr. Shea. My daughter will be coming home. We have a wedding to plan, after all."

"Father," Caleb speaks up, clearing his throat, "I really don't think we need to...."

"I did not ask you to think. I asked you to get your sister packed. We are going home, and she is coming with."

"Oh, no," I say, chuckling as all eyes swing my way in surprise. "No, Mr. North, you have that all wrong. You can go on and head home, and soon since you barging in here is not appreciated. Your daughter *is* home. Here, with me, is her home. Your son may follow commands like a well-trained pup," I cut a glare across the room at her brother, who ducks his head in shame. "Brielle *is not* your pet or your property. She is your *daughter*."

"Who the hell do you think you are?" he chortles, his too-small glasses sliding down his nose as he shouts at me.

"You know exactly who I am," I respond in a bored tone. "I am the man who is going to marry your daughter and if you ever want to see her or any grandbabies we will have, I suggest you learn how to talk to her. Until you do, let your pup see you out. Be careful, Mr. North, it's wild up here."

Brielle gasps as her father lets go a lengthy line of expletives. Her brother glances her way, and I can see he is not proud of being here. Not proud to be forced to follow any of his father's commands. This is all they have known. A father who tries to dictate the life he feels is best for them.

After all she has told me about her father, I do not doubt he loves her. I just doubt he knows how to let her go. How to let either of his children go. It sounded to me as if he loved his wife very much and when he lost her, I think just maybe he felt they were all he had left of her. He has tried to be careful with them, but really, he has just controlled them out of fear.

Her father filled my bunny with doubts no father should ever give their children. It was wrong of him. Wrong of her brother. They were meant to protect her. It was their job to make sure she felt safe, loved, and worth something. They failed at their jobs, but I will not fail her the way they did.

"Get out. Caleb don't let him do to you what he tried to do to her. And she loves you, please don't cut her off the way he threatened to."

"Threatened? You want to hear a threat? Hear this threat," her father puffs his chest up as he shouts at me, "that lodge the people told me you love so much. Consider it gone. You might have money and may think you have some power, but boy...cross me, and I will *show you* what real money and power can do. You will not take my family from me. I won't allow it."

"Daddy, stop it," Brielle speaks up at last. Her voice is strong, clear, but her eyes are sad, and I step back as she pushes at me. "Stop making threats. To me and to him. To Caleb. You cannot force us to live the life you want us to. If you want to be part of our lives, you have to let us choose our own lives. You have to let me make up my own mind. Can't you just trust me?"

I am proud of her as I watch her stand up to her father. So goddamn proud. The air is tense, and I wait for him to speak. Wait for him to cut her down as she tries to stand tall. But when she steps closer to him, I feel off. I am hit with panic as her and her brother seem to speak without words. Maybe I should not be shocked when she speaks, but a feather could push me over.

"I will come home with you," she says gently, her head bowing. "I know where I belong and I realize it's not up here," her voice breaks as she trails off.

"Brielle? What...what do you mean? How can you think that?"

Blood pounds in my head as she spins to face me, her guards back up. Her eyes are as distant as they were that very first day on the mountain. I can get past her guards again but not if she walks out with them. Not if she leaves believing that this is not where she belongs.

"I just don't want to keep faking it, Brett. We knew what it was. We were faking it, and you can fake things for a while but...not forever. I am so sorry I did this to you. That I made you...take care of me. I need to go back home where I belong. Because I *do not* belong here."

My heart stutters to a stop as she swipes tears away from her face. One simple sweep of her fingertips across her cheeks. There is something so final about the way she does it. As if clearing the slate. Giving up or starting over.

There is something behind her gaze that keeps me standing. That holds me back from losing it entirely. Something I am missing. But I am confused, and I am cut deep so I can't get to whatever it is. I cannot figure it out.

I watch her slip her coat on as her father and brother wait at the door. There are things of hers here, but she decides to leave them behind. To torture me, perhaps. Her shampoo in the shower, her panties in my drawers, her favorite sherbert in the freezer. None of it matters to her, I guess.

Brielle walks out leaving me and all her things behind.

Chapter Ten

Brielle

They say you always hurt the one you love.

Well, whoever said that is an asshole and I would like to punch them right in the pussy. Because I *know* a chick said that. I know some ice cold, wrecked and wretched woman said that shit. How do I know? Because I am just like that kind of woman because I just broke the hurt the one man I thought I could never hurt.

I hurt the man I love because he doesn't love me back.

Sitting in the back seat of a truck too big and too powerful for a brother who usually gets chauffeured around, I want to laugh. He looks so silly in his cashmere suit and expensive leather loafers in this big truck. My Brett might be a rich boy, but he earned that title on his own. He was never pampered or prissed up the way brother is. He would look right behind the wheel of this big truck.

Pain blooms in my chest as I glance back to watch the cabin sink into the darkness. The further away we get, the more it hurts. The more off kilter it beats. Clawing at my chest, I wish I could rip it out. It has never done me any damn good has it?

"We do not expect you to get married right away, sweetheart," father's tone is scarily soft, the voice he always uses after he crushes parts of me. "What with all you just went through, Greta and I understand you will need time to find the right husband. We just want you back with the family."

"I am *never* getting married. Tell your partners they can rent me for whatever rate you think I am worth. You and Greta can get fucked."

Beneath me, the truck, sways, and I gasp, clutching at my seatbelt. I figure the icy road caused the slide until I hear the chuckle. The truck slides off the road to just narrowly miss the mountainside. A chime dings and the cab lights come on, lighting up the dark road. Behind the wheel, my brother's shoulders are shaking, and I tear my belt off, afraid he is hurt.

"Caleb! Oh my god did you get hurt?"

"No more than you, Bri," he calls, twisting slightly to flash a smile. "I have never heard you talk to him that way. Not sure I ever laughed that hard. I am turning this beast of a truck around, Brielle. I am taking you home. Back where you really belong. Oh, and I am not getting married either. At least, not to that cold bitch Greta wants to sign our fortune off to. I will choose when and who I marry. And so will my sister."

"Caleb, I am coming with you. This is not my home. Brett and I were just...we were faking it. Just long enough for me to figure out..."

"Don't be thick, Bri. This is more your home than you have ever had. Finding you at a cabin, dressed as a bum," his voice softens as he turns to shoot a teasing grin at me, "cooking. You were cooking dinner for your mountain man. Jesus, you looked so normal, Brielle. So at peace and most definitely at home. Happy. Happier than I have ever seen you."

"I am happy here," I admit, eyes stinging with tears, "I was happy with him. I was going to tell you both. We were faking it, but I wanted to let you know that I was not faking it anymore. I....I love him, and I wanted to stay."

"Then why did you leave with us?" Caleb asks with a frown.

"Because she did not think I loved her," a gravelly voice calls out, startling me.

Turning, I see both the front and rear passenger doors on the truck thrown open. Father is pacing out in the snow, shouting into the wild winds. Snow is starting to come down and I tell myself for a moment that it is just shadows I see. The wind I am hearing. But it's not. I see him and then I can feel him.

"Br-brett?"

"Bunny...I ought to have known. For you to believe it, I need to say it. Not just show it or think it or even feel you. They said you like romance and I guess they were right," his voice is strong and clear despite the howling weather.

Pulling me from the truck, he cradles me against his chest, wrapping me in a blanket. Walking a few steps towards his jeep, he pauses. We almost get lost in the blowing wind and I feel as if it is just the two of us.

"I love you Brielle. I loved you the moment you slid down the slopes at my lodge. You need to hear it so I will always say it. They might have never said it, but I will, bunny. Because I love feeling it, I love having this. I love you, bunny. You knew but when I did not say it...."

"I thought it was fake," I whisper, bowing my head to roll my brow across his. "I would have let it keep being fake if you would have let me. I loved faking it. I loved being up on this mountain with you. I even loved faking it at all those parties. But when my father threatened the lodge and you never said you loved me, I just figured I had to stop faking."

"Your father could only take one thing from me that matters, bunny: you. I love you, baby. Always have. And I promise I always will."

"You never break your promises to me," I whisper, the words almost lost in the blowing wind. "I love you, Brett. I love you so much."

Brett's grin tells me he heard those words loud and clear. He bends his head and I meet him halfway, kissing him deep, soft, clinging to the moment as it swirls around us. Another of the little moments I wish we could capture.

"Come on, bunny. Let's get home. I think we might be snowed in if we get lucky," he teases, both of us chuckling as he rushes to his waiting jeep.

"Wait! My brother!" I shout, trying to wiggle from his grasp just as he sets me in the jeep.

"I will make sure they are both fine," he says gently, belting me in before he kisses my head. "Stay here, please, I don't want you getting lost in this snow."

Nodding, I let him close the door then turn to watch his dark figure rush across the road. I turn to keep an eye on him, turning up the heat to warm the Jeep. I bounce a knee as I wait, watching the darkness, hoping he comes back and tells me my brother is fine. And that my father is too, I guess.

"Yeah!"

I hear a shout, twisting back and forth in my seat to see where it came from. I shout when the driver's side door flies open and snow and icy air blow in. It's Brett and I cry out, trying to throw myself at him before my belt snatches me back. Chuckling, he reaches over, undoing my belt. He slips icy hands beneath my sweater, lifting me to draw me into his lap.

"Warm me up, babe. Your brother is coming back tomorrow. After he gets your father out of town. They were bickering when I loaded them, safely, back in that truck. Your brother is laughing his ass off. You really shocked the hell out of him. Also, he has no business driving that truck."

Laughing, I nod, pressing kisses all over his face. "I love you, Brett. I love you so much. Take me home. I want to warm you up a lot more."

"Oh yeah," He hums, tipping his head back as the dome light slowly starts to dim. "I am down for getting warmed up. First in that mouth and then in that sweet pocket," he teases with a laugh.

"Take me home, Ace," I say with my own laugh.

We argue about me moving from his lap until he gives in and lets me stay there. Only after I let him strap us both in—as if that is any safer. But he knows these roads almost as well as he knows my curves. I trust him. I trust him with my life and with my heart.

"We won't talk about tonight again," his voice is soft, calm. I press closer because I hate that tonight even happened. Or almost happened.

"I want to talk about it once," I argue as he takes a turn that slams me into him, "They never did tell me they loved me. Caleb tried to show it. My father...I think his love died with my mother. It just took all the good out of him, losing her. I had everything a girl could ever have. How could I want more? How could I be so selfish? That is why the causes and charities. Why I protest and march."

"To make up for wanting to be loved? For wanting what most of us want the most? Bunny, you were loved. You had your brother. I believe your father loves you the best he knows how to. Quinn, Lennon, some of those goddamn lumberjacks. And I love you. You were never being selfish. And you are always worthy of being loved. Of being happy."

Nodding as tears slip down my face, I snuggle closer. He has made me feel loved. Happy. He has made me feel at home for the first time. I don't want to run off to South America or Asia to march for something or save someone.

I just want to exist. Brett told me once that existing is enough.

When we get home, he carries me right to bed after locking the door and letting me know where his guns are. I laugh at that—it's not as if they were going to kidnap me. Well, not really. They gave me the choice and I chose wrong because I didn't know how to be loved. I didn't know what it looked like, really.

Now, as Brett spreads me out in bed and stands staring down at me, I know just what it looks like. I told him once that the way he looks at me, it makes me feel as if I make sense. And now I really get it. As he climbs over me, cradling me close as he sinks inside of me, I get it.

It makes sense because he loves me. He looks at me as if he loves me. And he knows I love him. Maybe I even did that day I crashed at his feet at the lodge. I am not sure about that—but I am sure that I love him now.

I am sure that I will always love him.

I am absolutely sure that I will never have to fake it.

Epilogue

Brett

One Week Later

Snowfall on Christmas ensures a perfect holiday.

Staring out over the snowcapped mountains as a slow snow falls, I am certain it will be a Christmas to remember. Snow has fallen for days but it just sets the perfect scene. Standing with a cup of hot cocoa, smelling my grandmother's recipe cookies baking, and hearing my bunny singing Christmas carols as she bounces around the kitchen is the kind of scene I want to live in forever.

Turning to watch her, I chuckle when she tips her head back, using the whisk as a microphone. Brielle catches me watching her and laughs too, shaking her head as she flushes pink. Crossing the room towards her, I stop just briefly to glance at the tree towering by the fireplace. Brielle spent all week making it perfect.

Her brother Caleb will be here later today as well as her best friends and a few other of our friends. Luke will be here with his wife Leia as well and the girls are excited to make their first Christmas dinner together. Before all of that gets started, we will spend our first Christmas morning together.

Last week was a turning point for us. When her father showed up and threatened my lodge if she did not leave with him, she left. There was no way I was letting her get out of Driftwood, but it took me a minute to get my wits about me. I realized after I watched her walk out of my cabin that I had done just what her father and brother had done to her.

I gave her things, gifts, a place to call home, even orgasms, but I had never said the words.

Hearing someone say I love you, hearing the truth in those words, it means something. It matters. Brielle doubted her worth for so long, partially because the most important people in her life never said those words. They tried to show it, sure, but sometimes words do speak louder than actions.

"You look beautiful playing homemaker," I tease her as I move behind her as she fusses with more cookies. "I love you, bunny."

Her little sigh every single time I say it to her tells me I am getting this right. I tried to play hero when her father cut her off, sweep her up to my cabin, take care of all her troubles, but that was not what she needed. Brielle is a strong, capable woman. One who faced down and fought adversity and tyranny—her father cutting off her money was never going to get in her way.

"I love you too, baby," she coos, making my chest bloom with emotions I am sure will just continue to get bigger, warmer, every time she says it.

"After you finish with those cookies," I start, reaching out to snatch up a warm, gooey one, "come open some presents. We can save some for later when the others get here, I promise," I tell her, biting into the cookie and letting out an appreciative moan as the chocolatey flavor fills my mouth.

Winding my arms at her waist, I pull her back against me and burrow my face against her neck. Brielle giggles and nods, moving with me as she finishes her task. Turning at the waist when the last cookie is on the plate, she smiles up at me with a beautiful, bright smile, her blue eyes sparkling.

"Might have a gift under there I want you to open to, Ace," her voice is teasing, a waggle of her brows making me laugh.

Bending, I kiss her pink lips, sighing into the kiss as it turns hotter, her body twisting to press closer. My hands move to sink into her thick, red hair, the silk strands pinned up atop her head. I pull gently at the tie holding it all out of her way, letting it spill over her shoulders.

"I got the gift I wanted most," I breathe the words at her jaw as I move my lips there, "I got you, bunny. What more could I want?"

Shaking her head at me because she loves when I go all soft for her, she pulls me from the kitchen towards the tree. We sit at the fireplace, her draped across my lap as I lean back against the warm river stones as the fire flickers beside us. I reach beneath the tree for the box I want her to open most.

Well, the thing I want her to have most is tucked away in the fuzzy white stocking she has hanging on the fireplace, but she will get that later.

"This is huge," she says as she slides from my lap to sit at the floor with the big box between her legs.

Staring down at her, I cock a brow and wet my lips because I can see up her cute red skirt. Her black lace panties hide nothing and reach out, diving my hand beneath her skirt. When I yank at her panties, pushing them aside, she gasps. I stroke her folds open just once, just seeing if she's as soft as she looks under that lace. And, of course, she is.

"You will get huge later tonight, bunny," I tease her as I bring my finger to my mouth, sucking off her cream with a loud pop.

"Behave! We will have guests later. Unless you want to fuck me beneath this tree right now, keep those filthy hands to yourself, Ace," she says it like she means it, but we both know she doesn't.

And I will be fucking her beneath that tree, no doubt about that.

For now, I just want to watch her open that gift. Her eyes shimmer in the lights of the tree, glowing bright. Slowly she lifts the lid off the big square box, setting it aside. Her eyes flick to mine, but I just wait for her to pull back the tissue paper. When she does, her eyes come back to mine and this time, they are brimming with tears.

"Oh...oh, Brett....baby," she coos, breaking off as her hand flies to her trembling lips. Lifting out the first snow globe, the one of a figure on skis lying in the snow with another figure standing over it, she knows just what it is. Our very first moment together, one she told me she wanted to capture.

"Keep going, bunny. There is more," I tell her, nodding at the box.

Brielle pulls out all ten of the snow globes one by one. Each one, she gushes over, touching all the fine details of the woodwork Landon did. All the colors are her favorite: soft pinks, grays, whites. Even the trees and glittery stars keep the same color scheme. As soon as she pulls out the very last one, she sniffles, wipes at her face and shoots to her feet.

Sitting back, I watch her do just as I hoped she would. Going to the fireplace, she sets each of them up, one by one. All in the order they happened. Our first meeting at Shea Lodge, to the night in the snowstorm when I told her I loved her last week. They fill the mantle, but we will add more, I have already told Landon he will have to make at least a dozen more for her.

Once she sets up the last one, she climbs back into my lap. Pulling at my hair gently, she fuses her mouth to mine and shows me with her lips how much she loves her present. I cradle her close and kiss her back, letting her know how much I love her. How much I meant it that she is the greatest gift I could have gotten this holiday.

I am about to get back to talk of fucking beneath the tree when a knock sounds at the door. I grumble and grouse, but I want her to have the best Christmas, so I let her go so I can answer the door. I watch her race back to the kitchen where she pulls on a cute apron and rushes to the stove.

"It will be the girls, I bet. They want to get started on our first real holiday in Driftwood."

Seeing her lit with excitement is just another gift. I love her so deeply, all I want is to make her happy. To be the person who gives her everything she needs. But I am not all that she needs. She needs this holiday with her friends and what is left of her family.

"Merry Christmas!" Quinn shouts the greeting as I open the door to find both her and Lennon waiting, hands full of bags.

"Happy Hannukah too, if someone celebrates that," Lennon adds as they stop to press a kiss to my cheek before they race to the kitchen.

Turning, I watch the girls embrace, laughing and talking fast about their plans for dinner. Brielle catches my eye and I can see how happy she is. And it makes me happy. At the door, I wait, seeing Quinn's husband Keller carrying a wicker basket full of gifts. Behind him, a grumpy looking behemoth of man stalks, also loaded down with gifts.

"Merry Christmas, Keller," I call to him as he shakes the snow off his boots and grins at me.

"Merry Christmas, brother," he replies with a booming shout and a cheeky grin. Glancing back at the big man behind him, he lets out a sigh. "This is Locke, my cousin and the new man up at the landing. Had nowhere to go for the holiday, so I forced him to come with us."

"Not a problem, brother," I say, meaning it as I send a nod at the big man. "Anyone is welcome here today, definitely if they are family."

"He doesn't do much but grunt and eat," Keller tells me with a chuckle as Locke ducks his head at me then heads inside towards the tree. "He is a bit of a loner. Couldn't leave him alone on the holiday."

Watching the loner lumberjack start unloading the presents, I smile. These big burly loggers keep Driftwood thriving, but they mostly keep to themselves. They are a close nit group of men, most of them having done military time together. Since we all live on the mountain, I am almost considered one of them, and I am grateful for the friendships I have built with Keller, Mack and the others. I am sure this Locke will be a friend too.

We head towards the fire as the girls talk and laugh in the kitchen. I take note of Locke watching every single move Lennon makes. The brash and loud woman is a ball of energy, tossing her raven hair and telling off color jokes as the girls make a mess cooking.

"Yeah, he has not taken his eyes off her since she showed up to come here," Keller says with a chuckle, nodding at his cousin.

Locke stands and continues to stare at the ladies. Well, his stare is focused on one in particular. When she stumbles on bare feet, he stomps the distance between them to catch her, making her laugh up at him. When he turns away, I swear I see the big guy blush.

Quinn brings us some beers and tells us to keep the fire going. That just means stay out of their way for a while as they work on dinner. None of these girls have done much cooking in their life so we stay at the ready, just in case something catches fire, or they chop appendages off.

After I open my beer, another knock sounds at the door and I go grab it. Caleb is there, almost consumed by the stack of presents he has piled up. I laugh and take some, telling him he went overboard. But I know he wants to make things up to his sister, so I suspect this is just the beginning.

No sooner do I start to shut the door than my Luke knocks, sticking his head in with a smile, towing a very pregnant Leia behind him. I let him in, and he joins the guys at the fireplace. It is the first time since my grandfather was alive that I hosted a holiday, and I am so happy to have everyone here.

While the girls cook, we sit at the leather couches near the fireplace, talking about the winter season and logging. I talk a little bit about the Lodge and Luke tells me he is excited for the promotions he has set up for the coming year. Keller talks about being married and getting kids going soon.

Once dinner is going, the girls all come join us by the fireplace. Soft holiday music plays as we open some gifts, drink spiked cider, and laugh together. Lennon gets us playing some games and the tipsier she gets, the closer Locke watches her.

Before dinner gets plated, I signal Quinn to grab the stockings. I set up one for the whole group, except Locke since he was a late addition. I laugh when Lennon sits right in his lap and offers to share hers. Quinn gives Brielle hers last and I take a deep breath before I stand to speak.

"I got a little something for all of you. Sweets, good brandy, a few small trinkets, and lifetime passes at Shea Lodge. For you, bunny," I pause a moment as I go to her by the fireplace, the same spot where she opened all the snow globes earlier.

Reaching in her bag, I grab the black velvet box. Kneeling, I almost chuckle when she gasps and covers her mouth. Popping open the box, I show her the ring and start again.

"We said we were faking this for everyone else to believe we were going to get married. It was never fake for me, Brielle. All those plans I talked about, weddings in Ireland or a private Island, that was wishful thinking. Me talking wishes out loud. Loving you was never fake for me and it was never just for the holidays. Marry me?"

Brielle's eyes shimmer with tears and she glows in the light of the Christmas tree. Her head shakes and my hand trembles around the ring. Then she slides to the ground in front of me. Reaching into her pocket on her cute apron, she pulls out a similar box.

"I made your grandmother's cookies so I could propose to you tonight. I was going to put your grandfather' wedding band on your glass of milk with a bow. Yes, Ace, I will marry you. I love you!"

"You sneaky little shit! I love you bunny. You can still propose with the cookies," I bend close to whisper at her ear, "later, when I am fucking you beneath this tree. Because I told you, you were the best gift I could have gotten this holiday. My bunny. My bride to be."

We kiss softly after she giggles at my dirty whispers. The others applaud, hoot, holler and shout congratulations. The girls gather around to look at her ring after I slip it on—though two of them were there when I picked it out. The guys clap me on the back and her brother tells me he will be there for the wedding and make sure her father is not.

Then we head to the dining room where the girls set beautiful place settings for dinner. Keller pours wine and Luke and I help carry the food out. Locke just hovers near Lennon, doing whatever she asks of him. We sit down together and the girls bathe in the praise we heap on them foe the beautiful meal.

It is our first holiday together, but I already can't wait for the next. For birthdays with her and Thanksgiving with these great people. I cannot wait to take her skiing down the bunny trail someday. And I cannot wait to see her round with our babies, hopefully by next Christmas.

We agreed to fake it for people to back off both of us for the holidays. But I always knew my Holi-date would become my forever date.

Thank You for Reading!

I hope you loved Brett and Brielle's Story! Please consider **leaving me a review**. Want to find out what happens with Lennon and Locke? Their story is available now! **Snowed in with The Lumberjack!**

Or maybe you want to know about Landon and Lilli? Read their sweltering story in **Summer Fling With the Lumberjack!**

And find out about Brett's best friend, Luke, as he falls in love with his soulmate, Leia, in **Mountain Man's Mix Up**.

And check out my **AMAZON PAGE** for details and give me a follow so you never miss a new release!

Join my newsletter for bonus material, first looks, and a FREE BOOK!

About Dee Ellis

Born and raised in the Midwest, reading and writing have always been Dee's passion. Short stories became long stories that finally, became books.

While playing grownup during the day, meaning working a job, Dee wrote her first book. When not reading or writing, which leaves less time than she's proud of, Dee loves spending her time with her furbabies, her husband and lots of movie nights.

Find Dee:

Reader Group: **Dee's Dolls**

Instagram: **@AuthorDeeEllis**

Twitter: **@AuthorDeeEllis**

TikTok: **@authordeeellis**

More from Dee

The Burn Series:

Let it Burn

Burn It Down

Burn for Me

Slow Burn

Crystal Cove Holidays Series:

Snow Angel

Stupid Cupid

Chasing Glory

Tricky Treats

New Resolutions

Lucky Duck

Good Fridays

Father Figures

Scary Single

Having Grace

True Ridge Series'

Tennessee Truckers Series:

First Run

Long Haul

Double Team

Big Rig

Good Buddy

Come Back

Driftwood Peaks Series'

Driftwood Lumberjack Series:

Hard Wood: Driftwood Peak Series #1

Cherry Wood: Driftwood Peak Series #2

Thick Wood: Driftwood Peak Series #3

Deep Wood: Driftwood Peak Series #4

Driftwood Wood You Series:

COMING SOON!

Wood You Dare: Driftwood Peak Series #5

Wood You Beg: Driftwood Peak Series #6

Wood You Come: Driftwood Peak Series #7

Wood You Knot: Driftwood Peak Series #8

Driftwood Mountain Men Series:

Mountain Man's Hideout

Mountain Man's Obsession

Mountain Man's Mix Up

Mountain Man's Sweets

Mountain Man's Fake Fiancé

Cocky Cocktails Series:

Maybe Mimosas

Maybe Margaritas-Coming Soon!

Maybe Martinis-Coming Soon!

Maybe Mojitos-Coming Soon!

5 Star Daddies Series:

Daddy Flyboy

Commander Daddy – Coming Soon!

Daddy Maverick – Coming Soon!

Sergeant Daddy – Coming Soon!

Bad Boys Worldwide:

Naughty Irish Sailor

Naughty British Boss

Naughty Italian Fighter

Naughty French Nerd – Coming Soon!

Naughty Arabian Prince – Coming Soon!

Naughty Scottish Rogues – Coming Soon!

Fellow Falls Series:

Ride a Cowboy

Texas Twister

Claimed by The Cowboy

Roped by The Cowboy – Coming Soon!

Pine Grove Passions Series:

80s Baby:

When I Think of You

Hurts So Good

Hot For Teacher

Step By Step

Harmony Hollow Misters Series:

Mr. Pink

Mr. Daring

Mr. Greed

Mr. Vows

Mr. Mess

Mr. Bossy

Mr. Flirt

Mr. Grump

Mr. Mile-High

Harmony Hollow Hawks Series:

End Game

False Start

First Down

Harmony Hollow Howlers Series:

On Thin Ice

Puck Luck

Iced Out – Coming Soon!

Totally Pucked - Coming Soon!

Sweet Treats Series:

Sweet Treat

Sweet Cream

Sweet & Savory

Sweet Memory

Sweet Tease

Sweet Fit

Sweet & Sour

Sweet Secret

Sweet Baby

Standalones:

Mustang Maverick

Miss Matched

Lucky Chance

Tempting Tutor

It Takes Two

Forgive & Forget

Bred by The Deputy

Flirt Club Series:

Dear Sexy Swimmer

Spring Break Heartache

His Sun Drop

Her Captain's Deck

Shore Thing

Royally Theirs

Teaching Ms. Tingle

Made in the USA
Monee, IL
11 February 2025